THE HART'S REST

WARRIORS OF THE FIANNA
BOOK FIVE

BY
SOPHIA NYE

ARE YOU SIGNED UP FOR DRAGONBLADE'S BLOG?

You'll get the latest news and information on exclusive giveaways, exclusive excerpts, coming releases, sales, free books, cover reveals and more.

Check out our complete list of authors, too!

No spam, no junk. That's a promise!

Sign Up Here

www.dragonbladepublishing.com

Dearest Reader;

Thank you for your support of a small press. At Dragonblade Publishing, we strive to bring you the highest quality Historical Romance from some of the best authors in the business. Without your support, there is no 'us', so we sincerely hope you adore these stories and find some new favorite authors along the way.

Happy Reading!

CEO, Dragonblade Publishing

ADDITIONAL DRAGONBLADE BOOKS BY AUTHOR SOPHIA NYE

Warriors of the Fianna Series
Song of the Fianna (Book 1)
Prince of Fire (Book 2)
Into the Ashes (Book 3)
Princess of Elm (Book 4)
The Hart's Rest (Book 5)

Also from Sophia Nye
Outlawed (Novella)

For Sorcha.

You were a far better dog than I deserved. I hope, wherever you are, you can finally run again. The late nights are so lonely without you.

I thought of you on every page, my forever writing buddy. This book is for you—the last one we started together.

THE WARRIORS OF THE FIANNA

Deep in the heart of the Kingdom of Munster, the legendary King Brian Boru has brought an ancient brotherhood back to life: The Fianna. Now entering his senescence, King Brian has all but achieved his dream of becoming High King of Éire, uniting the nine kingdoms to defend Éire's emerald shores from *Fin Gall* raiders. He will need the aid of the kingdom's best warriors to complete his vision and claim the seat of the High King.

But it is no simple task to become a warrior of the Fianna. Seven trials, the same seven used by the ancient Fianna, test the mettle of all who would claim such an honor.

Intelligence: Memorize the twelve books of poetry, so that you may be knowledgeable about the history, genealogy, and legends of your people.

Defense: With naught but staff and shield, defend yourself from nine men's spears while standing deep in a hole.

Speed: Outrun pursuers through a forest, without being injured. But take care! Not a branch may be broken to prove your skill.

Movement: Leap over a tree with a height to match your own, then crawl beneath a branch lower than your knee.

Recovery: Run through the forest with all speed until you step upon a thorn. Remove it without slowing down!

Bravery: Fight outnumbered without faltering.

Chivalry: Marry for love.

Truth in our hearts,
Strength in our arms,
Honesty in our speech.

CHAPTER ONE

April, 1002

CONAN STOOD IN the small solar at the fortress of Cenn Cora, waiting. He knew something had happened, or Brian, King of Mumhain and Conan's foster father, would have come sooner. He'd been invited almost a month ago now, but had only arrived this morning. The first thing he'd done hadn't been to visit his newborn great-niece, but to call a meeting.

The seven other men who stood waiting with Conan were the best men he knew. They'd all sworn an oath to Brian, completing a rigorous set of trials and forming a band of elite warriors—the Fianna. Their sole purpose was to act as his right hand on missions that proved too difficult or too delicate for the aging king or the average soldier.

Brian himself sat in one of the four chairs, frowning at the lot of them over a thick, grey beard. His blue eyes found first Conan, then his younger brother Diarmid, before finally landing on his older brother Cormac.

"Your father built a bridge," he declared. "A damned inconvenient one, at that."

Conan blinked. He must have heard that wrong. "Our father died this winter. I saw it with my own eyes."

Cahill, King of Connachta, had sired five children who yet lived. His eldest, Dunla, was Brian's young and devoted wife. Next was Teague, a rat of the highest order who had remained with Cahill and sided against Brian. It was best never to believe a single word that spewed from his mouth. Cormac, Conan, and Diarmid—all three Fianna who had served Brian since childhood—were the last three, in that order.

The king raised a crooked finger, one of many injuries from his fighting days. "You saw him fall into the sea," he countered. "You did not see his body."

"You cannot mean that old bastard survived the fall!" Diarmid cried. None of them liked their father, and that was putting it mildly.

"Impossible," Cormac agreed, calm and rational as ever. "It would've broken his bones, at the very least."

"How do you know?" Illadan, their leader and Brian's nephew, asked.

Conan knew the answer as soon as Illadan finished the question. There was only one way Brian could have learned such a thing—Teague, perhaps the least trustworthy man in Éire and, unfortunately, Conan's eldest brother.

"Teague sent a messenger a few days after you did," he told them. "I sent men north to investigate the validity of his news, and they found it to be true."

"They *saw* our father?" Conan pressed.

"They did," Brian grumbled. "But I'm more concerned about the causeway. He's blockaded us from the Sionainn."

Conan hadn't believed he could be more shocked than to learn that his father yet lived. But to build a bridge across the Sionainn would take immeasurable manpower and materials. In many places it was near a mile wide. "Where?"

"Ath Luain." Brian turned toward Conan. "Through the shallows so he could add posts more easily, I'd imagine. The men I sent said it's about three-quarters of a mile across at their estimation."

"Is it over the ford?" Cormac asked, thinking much the same as Conan. One of the most travelled fords across the Sionainn sat near Ath Luain.

Brian shook his head. "Just north of it."

Conan couldn't believe any of it. His father surviving a fall from a hundred feet or more into the sea was absurd enough. But then to imagine he recovered sufficiently to take another stab at Brian and build this causeway felt surreal. If Brian's men hadn't seen his father themselves, Conan would have been certain that Teague had made it all up and built the causeway himself.

"You told us he didn't miss the rocks," Conan recalled aloud. How could he have survived?

Brian shrugged, sighing. "That was how it looked. Teague says he broke many bones, but has healed enough to walk again. And plot against me, apparently."

"What do you want us to do?" Illadan asked, getting to the heart of the matter. "Do you want us to kill him?"

"I'd considered it," Brian began, "but it won't serve my interests best. We have Teague helping us, which lessens Cahill's threat. I need to focus on winning over the north and convincing Malachy to cede the kingship. If I were a younger man, I'd ride there myself and rid Cahill's body of his head for threatening my son's life. But my years grow longer as my time grows shorter. We must prioritize unification."

Several months ago, while they overwintered in Dyflin on a different mission, Cahill had kidnapped the king's son in an attempt to force his cooperation. While not an unheard-of tactic among the many kings of Éire, he was no less the bastard for it.

Conan was young enough and more than willing to exact vengeance on his king's behalf, but he knew what Brian was getting after. "You think making peace with them will prove the most effective way to gain the kingship," he guessed.

"I do. We've been using force for years in attempts to sway one another, and it has accomplished nothing but bloodshed along the borders. When we worked together, we took Dyflin and Laigin. I plan to travel north and convince Cahill and Malachy to confront Aodh with me."

"When do we leave?" Illadan asked. Conan knew he was already making plans. The man couldn't help himself.

"Broccan, Cormac, Conan, Diarmid and I leave in a few days. We will ride to meet Cahill and Malachy in Ath Luain and travel north into Ulaid from there. I've already sent messengers to request the meeting. The rest of you leave tomorrow, and when I return from the north, I expect that causeway to be gone. I leave the method and manner to your discretion, save that no one be able to link me or Mumhain to its destruction."

A leaden weight settled in Conan's stomach. He had been placed in the group traveling with his father and Teague. And the last thing he wanted was to see either of them again, let alone travel with them for weeks and pretend at civility.

"If it's all the same to you," he ventured, looking to his king, "I'd prefer to destroy the bridge."

Brian narrowed his sharp eyes, regarding Conan. "I'll allow it," he said at last. "Though I don't think you can avoid them forever, nor should you."

Conan inclined his head, knowing better than to argue with the man. Normally, he took every word of advice the aged king offered him. But he couldn't imagine what purpose it might serve to give either of them a moment more of his time.

"Now," Brian declared, rising slowly from his wooden chair, "I must see my great-niece."

Illadan, the father of the newest addition to the king's family, jumped to action, leading them all to the feasting hall at the heart of their holding in Cenn Cora. Inside, a circle of women sat before the fire, working on projects and talking softly amongst themselves.

Eva, Finn's wife, balanced a partly-sewn baby gown atop her swollen belly. Their child would follow its cousin near midsummer.

Niamh, Dallan's wife, tied herbs into bundles to hang in her stillroom. She stood when she spotted the men entering the hall, smiling at them warmly.

Ethlinn, Illadan's wife, cradled their daughter. Little fingers wiggled tellingly above the swaddling, a look of pure joy lighting

Ethlinn's face.

Cara, who had wed Conan's brother Diarmid, and Astrid, who had wed his brother Cormac, sat on either side of her, cooing over the wee girl. It was no secret that Astrid wanted children sooner rather than later. Now that Eva, her cousin, was carrying, Astrid could talk of little else.

"Let me see little Liadan," Brian called, walking to stand over Ethlinn and the babe. Gone was the stern king plotting against his enemies. In his place, a doting grandsire. Brian had always held a fondness for children—it was one of the things that Conan had found endearing in his own youth.

Conan followed behind him, peeking at Liadan over Brian's shoulder. She still hadn't much in the way of hair, but what little she had was fair as undyed linen. Her squashed, plump face was starting to show signs of resembling her parents, though to Conan she mostly looked like any other baby. He supposed if he ever had his own child one day, he'd be able to tell them apart.

"Has your mother come by to visit her namesake?" Brian asked Illadan as he took the swaddled babe into his own arms.

"Aye," Illadan smiled, never taking his eyes off his daughter. "She was here a month before the birth and only left a few days ago, and then only with great reluctance."

"Children are a blessing," Brian told him. "Don't squander yours."

Conan missed Illadan's reply, distracted by Niamh. Or, rather, Niamh's absence. And Dallan's, he noted, completing his scan of the hall. Leaving the rest of them to fawn over the babe, he ventured back out into the courtyard in search of his missing friends.

Niamh could not have children, though she and Dallan didn't talk about it often. It hadn't occurred to Conan until just now that all of this fuss over the baby might be difficult for them. As a skilled healer and midwife, Niamh had tended both mother and child for months and had delivered Liadan herself. She was always ready to watch the babe so that Ethlinn could get some rest. She and Dallan had done nothing but support their friends, but Conan realized that perhaps it hadn't been with as much ease as it appeared.

He found them sitting atop a low stone wall at the far eastern edge of the courtyard. Dallan's arm held his wife, a dark swath across her waterfall of golden hair.

Conan hopped onto the wall on the other side of Niamh, contemplating what he should say. A dozen or more ideas ran through his mind, but in the end he landed on blunt honesty.

"How are you doing?" he asked them both.

Niamh turned to him. Pale tracks ran down her cheeks, the only sign that she'd been crying. "I always knew it would be hard," she said softly. "It always *was* hard. I just didn't realize it would be this hard."

"The harder the battle, the stronger the warrior," Conan replied. "I don't think there are many who could do what you're doing with so much grace and strength, myself included."

"It's kind of you to say that."

Conan stood, facing them both. "I didn't say it to be kind. I said it because it's true, and I want to make sure you know it." He looked to Dallan. "Both of you."

He left them, not wanting to impose on their privacy. His vast experience with betrayal meant that he knew just how valuable the support of a true friend could be. No matter what, he'd ensure that his friends found that in him. The last thing he wanted was to turn into his wretched brother.

CHAPTER TWO

RAIN PELTED HER worn woolen cloak as Alannah forded the flooding road to reach Glasny's alehouse. It had been raining for days, spring breaking in full force and testing the integrity of the dikes along the River Sionainn. If not for the newly finished bridge, Alannah would've been soaked to her knees crossing the ford.

Heaving into the creaky oaken door, she threw it open and hurried into the alehouse and out of the gale. Glasny turned toward her, his deep blonde waves even wilder than usual today.

Glasny's alehouse was the most unassuming building in all of Ath Luain. It looked like a large cottage, with perhaps a bit of extra seating outside. No sign denoted it as anything other than what it seemed. Yet everyone in town knew it was the only place to go for a good ale and a sympathetic ear.

"I wondered what sort of depraved soul would come drinking as the sun yet rose," he grinned. He kept his beard short beneath a rounded nose and hazel eyes. His oval face was handsome and always friendly, and he'd been one of her father's best friends before the sickness took him.

"You have some of the best ale, but I'm afraid I can't drink while I'm seeing to business." Alannah walked over to the wooden counter where Glasny stood, handing him the coin he'd earned for helping find customers for The Hart's Rest. "We've had five guests in the last sennight tell us they came on your recommendation."

He took the money, stowing it beneath the counter. "The Hart's Rest is the best inn in Ath Luain," he shrugged. "I wouldn't have partnered with you if I thought otherwise."

"I'll be back next week," Alannah promised.

"I heard some interesting news last night." His deep voice teased. "The men are due back from the north any day now."

Alannah's heart stopped beating for a moment while her mind processed that. "You're certain?"

"As anyone hearing news from drunkards can be, aye."

Her brothers were coming home. It had been six years since they'd joined the king's forces to make enough money for the family to survive. Alannah and Emer had been on their own, starting the hostelry when the drought came through and ruined their pitiful attempt at farming two years in a row. Alannah had protected her younger sister, the only one left to do so. They'd managed to build a successful business on their own.

But they wouldn't be alone much longer.

"Thank you," she whispered with a smile. "Emer will be thrilled."

"As will I," Glasny sighed. "I'll finally get to stop worrying about them."

"That makes two of us."

Alannah had only one more stop to make before returning to her sister and The Hart's Rest. She could hardly contain her excitement at the knowledge that their brothers would finally be coming home, and Alannah knew Emer would feel the same relief—not that anyone would be able to guess that she ever despaired.

Alannah's little sister was a bright ray of sun on a frigid winter's day, bringing light and warmth everywhere she went. Emer might be four years younger, but Alannah looked up to her in that way, in how she always managed to see good where no one else did.

Crossing back over the bridge, Alannah found Nolan and Clíona in the market stalls near the center of the town. They traveled across Éire peddling holy symbols and trinkets, magical herbs and children's toys. *Everyone* knew Nolan and Clíona. They had grown children, though neither looked a day older than thirty-five. Well, except for the strands of grey peppering Nolan's dark hair. But his face held no wrinkles to match the changing colors. Clíona had deep brown hair that turned gold when the light caught it just right.

Much like Glasny, they partnered with Alannah and Emer in a mutually beneficial business agreement: in exchange for sending travelers to The Hart's Rest, they received a portion of the profits. With the new addition of the bridge, things were finally starting to look up.

Their cart held forth in the center of the market square of Ath Luain, piled high with bags and boxes. The small table they managed to fit into the cart sat before them, an array of trinkets spread to entice the curious customer.

"I take it that family found you, then?" Clíona asked, taking the small bag of coins Alannah offered her.

"They did," she smiled. "Thanks to you two. And a merchant who'd never been through town before."

"Glad to hear it," Nolan smiled back. "I'd much rather send folk your way than the alternative." He raised his dark brows emphatically, as if Alannah wouldn't know exactly what he meant.

'The alternative' was Oran, the closest the Devil had ever come to incarnating.

He also happened to have courted Alannah once, *years* ago, and did not take it well when Alannah refused to see him again. It wasn't her fault she saw straight through his good looks and into his black heart from the beginning.

When she and Emer opened The Hart's Rest, Oran decided that what the town really needed was yet another inn, but on the eastern side of the river so that he could grab folk on their way into town long before they knew The Hart's Rest existed. Alannah's pulse pounded angrily as she thought of all the business he'd stolen from them over the years, simply because she refused him.

Though it more than validated her decision, it caused their business to struggle until the bridge went up. Now, they stole that business right back from him thanks to easy access and a bit of promotion.

"I'm not sure that being better than the worst is really a compliment, Nolan," Alannah teased. "But I'll take it."

They all had a good laugh before Nolan raised his hand, trying again. "It's the best inn in the kingdom. Not because you do anything spectacularly different, but because it has heart. It has character. It has a real warmth, and that's not something everyone can create."

Alannah shook her head, shying away from the compliment. "That's all Emer," she admitted. It wasn't a jealous truth, either. Alannah could be calculating, cunning, and protective. She could plan the big ideas to move their business forward and keep things from getting rowdy when folks had too much ale. But Emer was the source of that warmth of which Nolan spoke.

Tossing a quick goodbye when a customer approached their wagon, Alannah hurried back to The Hart's Rest to share the good news with Emer.

The building itself was massive but outdated. The constraints of a limited budget had forced them to use the cheapest and most efficient materials. Alannah had worked until her hands bled to build that roundhouse and though it may not look like much, it felt like everything—the sum total of all their work for the past four years. A giant, physical symbol of their ability to survive even when the odds continued to stack against them.

As long as Emer was by her side, they were strong.

All of their guests had left that morn, giving Emer an opportunity to get a good cleaning done before more showed up today. At least, that was what she'd told Alannah as they broke their fast that morn.

So when Alannah caught the sound of a man's voice in the

inn as she walked up the drive, concern swirled up her spine. When the voice escalated to a shout, Alannah took off at a run. She closed the distance from the muddy road to the front door in record time, more than ready to draw the short sword she carried for just such purposes.

Before she opened the door, Alannah heard the man shout again and her heartbeat took off like a racing horse.

It was Oran. Emer was in there with Oran.

Alone.

CHAPTER THREE

THE LAST TIME Conan laid eyes on Ath Luain, he'd been a lad of seven summers, journeying south to foster with Brian alongside his older brother. As they approached the ford on the River Sionainn, the town looked larger than he'd remembered, though there was no great keep to cast shadows upon it like Caiseal or Cenn Cora. New buildings flooded the town like the river in spring, spilling across both shorelines and dragging freshly-dug roads along with them. The causeway came into sight as they crested the final hill on the path to the ford.

Apparently, Teague hadn't lied about the bridge.

But that didn't mean he wasn't a liar.

Dallan let out a low whistle. "That's one heck of a bridge. It's going to be a beast to light."

He wasn't wrong, either. Large enough to accommodate a cart and built of thick wooden timbers and planks, it stretched easily over half a mile to the western shore. They would need a suspiciously large quantity of oil and tinder to ignite it.

Illadan shot Dallan a look of warning. "Can you not hold your tongue in public?"

"I'd hardly call this 'public.'" Dallan gestured with both arms to the verdant fields and woodlands that blanketed the land as far as they could see.

"He's right. There's no one for miles," Conan jumped in, defending his friend. Not that Illadan wasn't his friend also, but he was much closer to Dallan and Finn.

Illadan frowned, but didn't argue. He spent more time with Cormac and Broccan, both of whom had traveled with Brian to deal with the other kings.

"And it looks like your brother was right," Ardál pointed out. He'd ridden much of the journey in his customary silence, scouting ahead and keeping to himself. Ardál's dark locks fell tamer than most of the other Fianna, in juxtaposition to his preference for the uninhabited wilds of the countryside.

"Maybe," Conan grumbled, his good mood gone. The last thing he wanted to think about was his villain of a brother. At least he had two good ones to compensate him for. "But just because the bridge is here, doesn't mean you should trust him."

"It won't be here for long," Dallan grinned, his eyes glittering with mischief.

Illadan pinched the bridge of his nose, reminding Conan of a parent surrounded by misbehaving children—which wasn't terribly far from the truth of their relationship with the Fianna's leaders. Most of the warriors had a knack for trouble, especially where women were concerned. "We stick to the plan," he ground out.

The plan, of course, being to pose as a band of traveling bards, as all of them were trained in poetry and Finn had trained as an actual bard before joining the Fianna. They would arrive a few days before Brian and his army, settle into an inn somewhere nearby, then scout the bridge and decide on the best plan of attack. They'd brought a supply of oil and tinder, but seeing the bridge looming large on the horizon, Conan doubted they carried enough.

The most important part of the plan was that they needed to remain undiscovered. Brian's entire revenge ploy depended on him *not* being culpable in the bridge's destruction. As best they could manage, it needed to look like an accident.

Whilst hotly debating the best placement of the tinder, they reached the outskirts of Ath Luain and were forced to cease their plotting aloud. Flooded muddy streets, reminiscent of the bogs of

Dyflin, made Conan glad of his horse. The buildings on the eastern shore of the Sionainn had multiplied in the years since he'd left for Mumhain. A veritable town had sprung where before there'd been just the smithy and the butcher.

One of the first buildings they passed was a large, rectangular wooden inn, built in the newer style that felt so different to the traditional roundhouse. A sign, carved into a wide plank and painted the yellow-green of birch leaves, showed a line drawing of a man lying down, clearly indicating the offer of respite. Beside it, stables stank of wet hay and horses.

"Let's secure a room, then we can have a look around." Illadan dismounted, moving in the direction of the inn.

Dallan and Finn followed him. Conan stayed outside with Ardál to guard the horses.

A handsome couple of middling years perched atop a merchant's cart, pulled their mare to a halt beside the men.

The man leaned down, his voice pitched away from the building. "You lookin' for a room?"

"Aye," Conan replied, uncertain what the man was after.

"The Hart's Rest is the only place to stay worth the coin." He tilted his head toward the bridge at the far side of the smattering of buildings. "Cross the river. It's at the far western edge of town. You can't miss it. Tell the girls Nolan sent you and they'll take care of you."

"What of this place?"

The man frowned at the building behind Conan. "I'd not stay there."

Conan nodded in thanks as Nolan gave the reins a good snap, setting his cart back into motion. "There must be some competition between them," he mused aloud to Ardál.

Ardál shrugged. "Or he really likes the other place."

Illadan, Finn, and Dallan returned from inside. Tension surrounded them like a cloud.

"There's no one there," Illadan grumbled, sounding more like Broccan than himself.

"I heard there's another hostelry on the far side of town," Conan offered.

Illadan mounted his horse, still grim. "Let's go."

The decision made, they started across the causeway. The structure was sturdy and well-crafted, which would only make their work more difficult. And, perhaps most concerning, several buildings sat in close proximity. Even the market square was within sight. They'd have to plan carefully.

As Nolan had promised, a giant roundhouse lay in the last row of buildings. A sign hung above the door, a deep green border surrounding a white hart. But the building and the sign and even the road beyond disappeared from thought as the door flew open and a furious man stumbled through it.

He looked of an age with Conan, handsome but for the scowl on his beet-red face, with cropped ash brown hair and a slim build. Conan disliked him instantly.

The man opened his mouth to speak, but was interrupted by a gorgeous woman using oaths so colorful he couldn't suppress a shocked laugh.

"Do. Not. *Ever* come here again," she seethed, "or the next time you'll walk out a eunuch."

"I think I'm in love," Conan laughed.

Not only could she put obnoxious men in their place and swear like his grandfather, she was stunning. Hair as dark as coal fell loose from a wide plait that lay over her shoulder. Two sapphire eyes leveled a challenge at the man from her oval face. And, as though that weren't enough to get his attention, she wore trews and a sword.

This was no simpering lass. She was a woman—a woman Conan was now *very* interested in.

"That can't be one of the 'girls' Nolan mentioned," Finn laughed.

The red-faced man lunged at her, throwing a punch that she narrowly dodged. Inside the inn, another woman screamed.

Conan swore, charging to intervene. He felt Illadan on his

heels as he sprinted the last leg of the path up to the inn. Finn and Dallan moved past the brawl to check on the woman inside. Ardál disappeared from sight.

Before Conan reached them, the woman threw a god-awful attempt at a punch instead of reaching for the sword hanging from her waist. Noble of her, but far less effective.

The man charged her again, but this time Conan caught his fist. Shoving hard, he propelled the man several steps backward.

"Get out of my way!" the man roared. "This doesn't concern you."

"If you don't have a damned good reason for attacking this woman, it most certainly does concern me," Conan growled.

The woman shot past him, fists flying at the man. "Go back to your own inn and leave my sister *alone!*"

Conan's pulse rose so fast he could hear it in his ears. *His own inn.* This must be the missing innkeeper. He'd been here harassing these women instead of minding his own business. It seemed Conan's instant dislike of the man hadn't been far from the mark.

She slammed her shoulder into the man's stomach. The force drove him back down the path a commendable distance before he landed another blow. His elbows dug into her back, forcing her to stand and face him.

This was getting out of hand. Conan grabbed the woman's arms, bracing her against him so that she couldn't continue the fight. Illadan grabbed the man.

"Alright," Conan shouted over their continued bickering, "now will *someone* please tell me what is going on here?"

CHAPTER FOUR

"LET ME GO!" she screamed, wrenching and kicking to free herself from the giant's grasp. "I can't punch him if you're holding my arms!"

"Aye, lass, that's the idea," the man chuckled. His hands held her arms in an iron grip. His feet didn't even shift as she thrashed about like a wild animal.

"Who are you and what's your business?" the other man demanded of Oran.

"He owns the other hostelry, near the river," Alannah answered, not trusting Oran to do it honestly. "He came here to harass my sister, and I kindly showed him the door."

"Is that the truth of it?" Oran's captor pressed.

"They're slandering my inn!" Oran whined.

"I can't be slandering your inn if I never speak of it," she spat back. "And stay the hell away from my sister!"

"How exactly is your hostelry running if you're not there?" The man holding her asked, his voice dangerous. "Is it worth losing business to harass a woman?"

"She's not a woman, she's a menace." Oran pinned her with a murderous glare.

And to think she'd ever considered courting the bastard. Clearly, her instincts could not be trusted. "Says the devil himself," she snorted.

"Let's get you back to your inn." The giant holding Oran put a heavy hand on his shoulder, steering him toward town.

The man behind her let go, finally giving her the opportunity to round on him.

"I was handling it just fine." She didn't even try to contain the anger that bubbled over into her tone. "I didn't need your help. Indeed, you only got in the way."

Heaven and hell, she'd wanted to punch Oran square in the face. But Alannah wasn't as skilled at fist fighting so she hadn't managed it before the men had broken up their brawl.

"I know." The man fought a smile, which only irritated her further.

"And now you're laughing at me." She threw up her arms in frustration. "Wonderful."

His handsome face sobered. Eyes the color of a thundercloud captured her full attention. "I'm not mocking your skill. I'm surprised and amused by your tenacity."

Her bluster deflated. "Oh."

"You had things well in hand when we arrived," he continued, taking a step toward her. "And I've no doubt you could've handled it. I simply can't sit idly by and watch a man attack a woman, no matter how well she can defend herself."

"Well next time let me do it myself."

"Next time?" He shook his head. "I don't think there will be a next time."

"There's *always* a next time." Alannah drove a finger into his hard chest. "And next time I expect to be allowed a fair fight. I'm not the one who needs to be rescued."

He put his hands out in surrender. "You have my word. If there is a next time, it belongs to you."

She nodded at him, finally backing down. She took a long look at the man. He was several inches taller than her, and she was tall for a woman. His dark, unkempt hair was tied back, his beard worn short. He seemed built of solid muscle. Dangerously handsome, this one. "Who are you?"

The man grinned, a look that brought a flutter to her stomach. "Conan. My companions and I were hoping you might have a room available."

One of those companions approached from behind the inn. "I didn't see anyone else," he told Conan.

"It was just Oran," Alannah assured them. "He was inside with my sister when I arrived."

The storm rolled back over Conan's face. "Did he hurt her?"

"He did not." Emer's bright, cheery voice called from the doorway. Two more giants walked out behind her. "And we do have a room open."

Alannah eyed the four men, still unsure what to make of these new arrivals. "What brings you to town?" They might have stepped in to help chase Oran off, but between their fit, towering statures and the array of swords, bows, and spears, they looked like trouble. And the last thing she needed was more trouble.

"We're bards, miss." The tallest one, with hair the color of summer oats, stepped forward. He had a kind, gentle face in spite of his height. "My name is Finn. I've spent much of my life training and traveling through Mumhain, but I wish to travel to the rest of the kingdoms as well."

"You don't look like any bards I've seen," Alannah replied, eyeing his sword meaningfully.

"When you're on the road as much as we are, you need to be able to defend yourself," Conan explained. "Too many cutthroats running about the hills."

That made sense, at least enough to lower her suspicions. "The weapons stay in your room," she told them, crossing her arms and standing straighter. She still couldn't believe how these men dwarfed her. "Will you be performing for us, then?"

"As often as you'd like," he promised. "You've already met Finn and I. And that's Dallan." He pointed to one of the shorter giants, with dark, shoulder-length hair.

"Ardál." The shortest of the giants inclined his head, though still several inches taller than her. Ardál also had dark, wild hair like Conan, but he kept it to his chin. His face reminded her of a fox, beautiful and cunning.

"And I'm Illadan." The man who'd escorted Oran back strode toward them down the path. "It's good to see that you take the safety of your establishment so seriously."

"It's my job," Alannah replied simply. "Believe me, you'd not want me to be the one doing the cooking." And once their brothers were gone, it became painfully clear that someone would need to keep order at the inn and drunken men's hands away from her sister.

She led the men inside, grabbing a broom to sweep up the shards of broken vessels—casualties of their confrontation with Oran, the bastard. She smiled as she recalled breaking it on his shoulder. He'd deserved it, too, laying hands on Emer like that.

Emer's sweet face lit up into a sunny smile as the men trailed inside. "How many rooms would you like?"

"Just one will suffice," Illadan answered, reaching for a coin purse on his belt.

Her sister took the coins he offered, far more than needed. "How long will you be staying?"

"Let's call it a month."

"That's a lot of coin to spend in one place," Alannah commented, her suspicions returning. "You must make good money to expect to make that back."

Conan grinned at her as Illadan paid Emer. "We are excellent at what we do."

"Then I look forward to hearing you play tonight."

CHAPTER FIVE

T HE TEMPESTUOUS BEAUTY turned, leading them across the feasting hall toward the far door. Due to the tumultuous manner of their arrival and introduction, Conan hadn't paid much mind to the guesting house itself until this moment.

The feasting hall was built in the old style, much like Brian's own hall. Except where Brian's fortress was a relic of the ancient past, the hazel branches and oaken thresholds of The Hart's Rest looked freshly made. Many of the roundhouses yet remained in Éire, but just as many had been replaced with the rectangular stone homes that grew in popularity with each passing year.

Conan couldn't help but notice the fine form of their hostess. She wore trews and léine, as a man would, though women on occasion wore them when they needed more ease of movement. The trews hugged her round hips and emphasized the tempting legs beneath them. The léine was regrettably loose-fitted, but even its generous size couldn't completely hide the dip of her waist. He couldn't take his eyes off her.

"You still haven't told us your name," he reminded her as they passed the central hearth, the beating heart of the hall. It crackled at him like an old friend.

"Alannah," she called over her shoulder. "And my sister is Emer."

"Did you build this hall?" Conan couldn't contain his curiosity.

"We did." She kept walking, passing the last of the eight

trestle tables that lined either side of the hearth.

Beside Conan, Dallan pulled up short, taking a long look around the room before hurrying to catch up. "You built a new roundhouse?" Dallan asked.

"Well, I would've preferred to build a fortress with two stories and all manner of antechambers, but money exists, and we hadn't enough for that." Her words fell like needles, prickly and sharp. "And we had to build it ourselves. I can weave hazel branches for months, but carting stone would've required help."

"You did a fine job," Conan told her, hoping to undo any insult taken. "It was a clever way to build something grand with less investment."

Alannah stopped before she walked through the door and back outside, sighing in a manner that reminded Conan of Illadan. "I realize the style is somewhat antiquated, and perhaps not to your liking. We have four small cottages of the same style as the hall, or one larger stone cottage in the current fashion. If you've no need of a separate space, we have cots in the feasting hall that you can use."

"I think we would prefer to share one larger space, if it's all the same to you," Illadan answered.

Conan knew it was so that they could plot with greater secrecy. Hopefully Alannah didn't take further offense by his request.

He watched the sway of her hips, hypnotic as a dancing flame, as they followed her around the outside of the domed feasting hall. It had been a while since he'd bedded a woman. Not so long as Broccan, of course, but he'd never been so free with his affections as Diarmid, either. Like Diarmid, though, Conan always ensured the woman understood that it was nothing more than a diversion for them both.

It wasn't that he was wholly opposed to marriage as Diarmid had been—indeed, he saw how happy his friends had grown as they slowly accumulated wives of their own. He simply hadn't yet found the right woman. And after his experiences with first his father and then Teague, Conan wasn't quick to trust just anyone.

Alannah led them to the left, following the gentle curve of the waist-high wattle palisade she'd no doubt built. The woman had tenacity, he'd give her that. They passed the four smaller domed roundhouses she'd mentioned, with the typical low entry and thatched roofing that reminded Conan of something vague yet familiar, a memory hovering just beyond reach. Passing through a large, empty space of patchy grass and mud, Conan spotted the stone cottage at the far end of the enclosure. They'd come nearly back to the front of the hostelry.

"Emer will start serving dinner within the hour. I suggest eating sooner rather than later if you'll be playing for us tonight. We tend to be full up for meals. If you need anything and you can't find me, you can come by our cottage." She pointed across the courtyard to the other side of the holding.

Conan saw only a stable and a pigpen, with some chickens running amok between them. "You live in the stables?" he teased, grinning so she knew he asked in jest.

"Our cottage is to the right, if you leave the hall by the back door. But you're welcome to see if the horses can help instead." Not waiting for a response, she walked past the men and the cottage, reentering the hall through the front doors.

"I like her." Conan's gaze followed her until she was out of sight.

Illadan frowned at him, opening the door to the stone cottage. "You're not seriously considering bedding the woman who's renting us a room?"

"I'm not considering it," Conan grinned. "If she's interested, then I'm planning on it."

"We just got here!" Illadan grumbled.

"All of you," Conan narrowed his eyes from one man to the next, "are married. I wouldn't expect you to understand."

Ardál crossed his arms. "I'm not."

Conan pointed a finger at him. "Yes, but you, I don't understand. You should be having fun with the rest of us unwed brutes."

Illadan rolled his eyes, ducking into the cottage and apparently giving up on reforming Conan. The inside was dark, but cozy. There was but one window, on the short wall farthest from the door. The rectangular building spread no more than twenty feet long and about half as wide. Oaken planks ran its length, a better floor than Conan had expected for a woman so keen to save coin. In the center, a small hearth sat cold and unlit, but would provide enough warmth and light for the chilly nights. Six pallets took up much of the floor space, three on either end of the cottage.

Conan walked the length of the building, running his hands across the rough stones. He'd put in countless hours of manual labor in his life, but something about this place impressed him. Alannah had built all of this herself. For some reason that thought captivated him, filling his mind with a thousand questions.

"Are you suddenly taking an interest in construction?" Dallan asked. "You've built homes and halls before."

He was right, of course. He'd helped build homes whenever folk needed it. He was a prince, after all, and he took care of his own. This past winter, the Fianna had all helped build halls to house guests for a tournament in Dyflin.

Conan shook his head, hoping to clear it. "Something about this place feels different." He turned to his companions, who regarded him with varying degrees of concern and amusement. "Perhaps it's just strange returning to Connachta after all this time."

"Perhaps you do need a good bedding, after all," Dallan mused.

"Whatever you do, don't lose us our room," Illadan warned. He set down his pack and grabbed his bodhrán. "And *do not* give away our identities."

When they returned to the hall to dine, they found a small crowd had already arrived for the meal.

"Have a seat, gentlemen, and I'll bring your dinners right over." Emer's smile, genuine and bright, could've warmed the coldest day.

They sat down at the nearest table, stowing their instruments beneath it. Alannah was nowhere to be found, but Conan had all night. He wasn't in any hurry. True to her word, Emer delivered a hot barley vegetable stew in trenchers of freshly baked oat bread. The rich, salty, nutty aroma that wafted from the food set his stomach grumbling. The men thanked her, then proceeded to devour the delicious meal. Two bites in, Conan realized why they had so many dinner guests—it was easily the best stew he'd ever had.

When they'd finished their meal, Emer set them up on the side of the hall opposite the kitchen, where there was enough space to set five chairs for the men to sit and play. By then, the eight tables were filled with diners. Emer moved about the room delivering food and refilling ale, chatting with folk and hosting the meal masterfully. Even if Oran hadn't been such a bastard, Conan could now easily see why The Hart's Rest was the best hostelry in town.

Though all of the Fianna could play instruments and perform poetry, few had voices for singing and none had a voice like Finn's. He could ensnare an audience from his first word, holding them captive until the last note slipped from his lips. Conan had seen it hundreds of times since they'd begun training together, and still Finn's skill amazed him.

They all played a few songs together, the ones they enjoyed most, the ones that encouraged folk to sing along. By the time the dinner ended, the dancing had begun.

And Conan had finally spotted Alannah.

Setting down his harp, he grabbed two ales from Emer and walked to stand beside Alannah. He thrust one of the ales at her.

"I thought you could use some company," he grinned.

She ignored the ale, her eyes scanning the room like a hawk tracking mice. "I can't drink that. I'm working."

He set her drink on the nearest table, taking a long sip of his own. "What does 'working' involve?"

Her head dropped toward him, blue eyes hitting him with

shards of ice beneath inky lashes. "I'm keeping watch."

"Keeping watch over—?" Conan let his gaze sweep the room. It seemed a normal feast, and far tamer than some of the alehouses he'd visited.

"My sister." She'd returned to scanning the room.

"She seems to be handling the crowd well."

"So long as the crowd doesn't start 'handling' her," she grumbled.

That was oddly specific. Given Alannah's state of alert, Conan wondered if this was a regular occurrence, like Oran's visits, apparently. "Has that happened before?" he asked.

Alannah turned to him again. "Often enough that it's my job to keep men's hands off her. Between her warm disposition, kind heart, and stunning appearance, my sister is something of a catch. Throw in her talent at cooking—" Alannah shrugged.

Conan nodded, narrowing his eyes at her. "And what of yourself?"

She jerked her chin in surprise. "What of me?"

"Seeing as you have an equally stunning appearance, I imagine you would have much the same trouble."

She blinked at him. "Are you..." Inhaling sharply, she tried again. "What are you even doing over here?"

Conan's confidence came dangerously close to faltering. "Isn't it obvious?"

Alannah's eyes fell from his face, instead landing just behind him. The change in her was instant, her look murderous.

Turning to see what had caught her attention, Conan felt his own blood boil. In place of amusement, he felt rage sweep through his bones. In the darkest alcove of the room, a very large man stood with his back to them.

Pinned between him and the wattle partition, was a wide-eyed Emer, pleading with them for help.

CHAPTER SIX

EOGHAN. HE DIDN'T come by every night, or even every sennight. But about once a fortnight, he made his way from his farm a few miles outside Ath Luain to try to harass Emer into becoming his wife.

His *second* wife.

Of course, it was in keeping with the law codes, and not entirely unheard-of. But Emer was too good for any of the men Alannah had met—marrying only to become the second wife of a man old enough to be their father was out of the question. And that wasn't even taking into consideration that as a hospitaller with her own homestead, Emer thoroughly outranked Eoghan and would be marrying down in every conceivable way. Preparing for her second fight of the day, Alannah stormed toward Eoghan and her sister.

But Conan got there first.

The charming rogue of moments earlier was gone. Before her raged a man who once more made her question what manner of bards looked and behaved as they did. He towered over Eoghan, staring him down with a look that made her mouth go dry. Being handsome and friendly was one thing. Defending her sister without question was another entirely.

And he wasn't only defending Emer. Nay, Conan looked as furious as Alannah felt, watching Eoghan's grubby hands reach for her sister's waist. Watching him lay into Eoghan, Alannah decided that perhaps she'd have that ale with him after all.

Though it was beyond her why he'd want her instead of Emer. The men always wanted Emer, and Alannah could hardly blame them. Her sister was the definition of feminine charm.

"I believe the lady would like to move." A threatening timbre threaded Conan's voice.

Alannah's fingers itched to reach for him. Instead, she wedged herself between Eoghan and Emer. "Eoghan, get out," she ordered, fighting whatever odd reaction she was having to their newest guest.

Eoghan rounded on her, his face ruddy from too much ale. He must've been drinking before he arrived, for Emer would never overserve him, knowing his poor manners.

"I've acquired more cattle," he slurred. "And I wish to take her to wife."

"My sister will never marry you," Alannah told him for the hundredth time.

Eoghan grabbed Alannah's arm, yanking her out of his way. "Let her speak for herself."

Conan moved so quickly she didn't have time to react. In one swift motion, he pinned both Eoghan's arms behind his back, spinning him away from Alannah and Emer. He leaned forward, his jaw taut as he whispered in Eoghan's ear. "You do not touch her."

A thread of desire tightened through her. Alannah hadn't been interested in a man in years, and *that* was what did it? Lord, perhaps she'd waited too long. She never imagined herself in need of a defender, not like her sister, but she had to admit that she greatly enjoyed watching Conan take on the role. To her increasing pleasure, he kept going.

"You do not touch either of them." He looked to Alannah, his slate eyes hard as stones. "What shall I do with him?"

"Toss him out. And remind him he's no longer welcome here."

Alannah couldn't suppress a smile at the way Conan paraded Eoghan across the hall, clearly enjoying his task of taking out the garbage. When they'd left the hall, she turned to Emer. "Are you alright?"

Her sister smiled. "I was about to ask the same of you. I can't remember the last time you *let* anyone help you."

Alannah snorted. "It wasn't as though I could stop him. You saw how he is."

"I saw how you looked at him," Emer sang, stepping right back into the role of hostess, as though she hadn't nearly been assaulted.

"And how was that?" Alannah folded her arms across her chest, following Emer toward the kitchen.

Emer picked up two trenchers that she'd already prepared. "With interest."

Alannah didn't know how to respond. She wasn't about to deny her interest in Conan, but she wasn't about to admit it either. In the end, she was rescued once more by the man in question.

Conan walked over to them, his intensity setting her desire aflame once more.

Good Lord. She needed to get control of herself. Alannah couldn't remember the last time she'd actually lusted over a man. Well, on second thought, she could. And that memory alone was enough to return her to her good sense. How had she been so wrong about Oran?

Conan took up a position beside her, within easy sight of Emer.

She should thank him for his assistance. Alannah opened her mouth with the intent of doing just that. But when his stormy grey eyes captured hers, her mind turned to mush. "What are you doing?"

"Working." The word fell from his lips lightly, dancing between them like a lure.

Alannah moved closer. "You don't have to do this."

"I know." He turned away from her, watching her sister squeeze through a growing crowd of dancers. "And neither should you."

Alannah stared at him, entranced. "It *was* obvious what you were doing," she said after some time, answering his question prior to their confrontation with Eoghan. "But this is working better."

The ghost of a smile flitted across his lips. And heaven help her, she wanted to kiss it right off.

AT THE TOLL of the next bell, the other four men stood and stretched, setting aside their instruments and chatting while folk filed out of the hall. Alannah helped Emer wash dishes in the buckets they kept in the kitchen. They served as much of the food on trenchers of bread as possible, but there was no way of serving ale without cups. Emer's constant surreptitious glances, accompanied by smirks, finally wore down Alannah.

"What?" she demanded, washing the last cup.

"He keeps looking at you." Her sister could barely get the words out without dissolving into girlish giggles.

Alannah rolled her eyes at Emer, but her chest rose nonetheless. "He's probably looking at you," she countered. "Whoever *he* is."

"You know very well who *he* is. He was trying to charm you, I think, helping with Eoghan. You should thank him properly."

If Alannah had been eating, she would have choked. "You must be joking."

"They're all handsome as the devil himself," Emer pressed, still grinning like a fool. "And you're not getting any younger."

It wasn't an insult. It was a fact. At twenty-seven, Alannah had long since accepted her fate.

"I'm not marrying, Emer. You know that." Over her dead body would her baby sister be left defenseless and running this inn on her own.

"You don't have to give up a husband on my account. And you don't have to marry him to thank him."

"What is it you're suggesting, little sister?" From the blush on

Emer's face, Alannah knew precisely what her sister was after.

Emer shrugged her delicate shoulders, rising and picking up the bucket to dump the dirty water. "I can survive on my own for a night. You should have some fun."

"Fun," Alannah repeated dubiously.

"Oh, for heaven's sake. Gentlemen!"

Every head snapped toward her.

Emer marched over to the men, the bucket sloshing with each step. She looked comically tiny in the forest of giants. "Were you planning to retire for the night, or are you up for some games?"

Her sister's infectious grin spread to all five of the men.

"Absolutely," Conan answered, his gaze moving to Alannah.

Her ridiculous sister then had the gall to turn and pin Alannah with a look that clearly said *I told you so*. Unbelievable.

But she wasn't about to be the one ruining the fun. Throwing her hands up in defeat, she picked up the clean cups she'd just put away. "I'll get the knucklebones and some ale."

CHAPTER SEVEN

LAUGHTER ERUPTED AS Dallan dropped the knucklebones again.

"I've never seen you so deep in your cups that you can't play properly," Conan snickered, smacking his friend's back while Finn swapped Dallan's ale for water.

"How dare you!" Dallan protested, a sloppy grin sliding around his face.

"It's for my wife, not you," Finn assured him. "She'll kill me if you die of drink."

"You're married?" Emer turned a curious look to Finn, her head tilting and bringing her black locks with it.

"Aye," Finn replied, giving Dallan a shove, "to his sister."

"And I'm married to *his* sister," Illadan added, pointing at Finn.

"She just had their first child," Conan offered, knowing Illadan would never boast but it needed doing. He'd seen the look on Illadan's face whenever he held that little girl. "Liadan."

Emer aahed just as he expected from any woman who heard about a new baby. But Alannah simply nodded her congratulations. She was unlike any woman he'd ever met, and not just because she dressed like a man. He couldn't put his finger on it, but she *felt* different, she moved through rooms and conversations like a queen, like she had complete control and she knew it.

"Are you all married?" Emer asked, looking from one man to the next.

"Ardál and I aren't," Conan answered with a pointed look to Alannah. He was going to crack her shell if it killed him. He'd made excellent progress since they'd started their game, but she was a challenge and he was more than happy to accept. He didn't miss the conspicuous elbow bump that Emer gave Alannah's side after he answered.

Alannah grabbed the knucklebones and tossed her hand, catching them in spite of being three drinks deep into the night. For a woman who seemed so in control, she played awfully coy with what he felt was clear interest. Perhaps she genuinely didn't return it.

But there was only one way to find out.

"Do you know how to use that sword you carry?" he asked as she made her next toss.

She dropped it.

He rolled his lips to keep from laughing at the fury that speared him from her sapphire eyes. She could glare at him all day if it meant those gorgeous eyes were on him.

"Why would I carry it if I can't use it?" She passed the knucklebones to Emer, her eyes never leaving Conan.

"To discourage trouble." He crossed his arms and leaned away from the table, looking as cocky as he could to prick her temper into action.

"Yes, I can use it."

"Show me."

"I could demand the same." She crossed her arms to match his.

In spite of her trews, sword, and fire, she still looked every inch a woman, down to the strong but feminine shape of her arms, folded in defiance. He'd never dare to call her a girl. He doubted the word could ever even slip out on accident, for there was no mistaking the difference in her.

Conan rose, unable to keep the grin off his face. "Happily." With a spring in his step at the thrill of the chase, he headed to his room to retrieve his sword.

"You know he's after you," Dallan slurred, clearly having lost his sense of decency with one of his cups of ale.

Alannah's chest felt like it was filled with air, like it could take off into flight, even though she knew that was a ridiculous notion. "I highly doubt that."

Why on earth would he chase her when Emer was such a catch? Petite, demure, a veritable ray of sunshine, and easily the prettiest girl in Ath Luain with her round face and dark hair. Not to mention her sister could cook well enough to serve a king. Her hand pies were legendary.

Oran was the only man who'd gone after Alannah, and he was clearly insane.

Alannah was skilled in many ways. Charming men wasn't one of them.

But a round of sparring with someone who, by the looks of it, could prove a true challenge, sounded promising. Her brothers had been gone for six years, and even though she could convince Glasny to go a round or two on occasion, she was sorely out of practice.

Conan returned, sword in hand. He carried it like an extension of himself, as though it weighed nothing when Alannah knew perfectly well that a blade that size would be exhausting to wield without constant practice. Perhaps they were a band of mercenaries who'd retired as bards?

Shaking her head, Alannah gave up trying to make sense of their odd guests for the evening. If they were staying a month, she'd have more than enough time to figure out why they could fight like warriors but play like bards.

"Have *fun*," Emer told her as she stood to follow Conan out the door.

She took him to the small patch of dirt behind the barn where she practiced the skills she needed to protect Emer.

The days of rain had turned it into a mud pit, her calfskin boots squelching and popping with each step. Sword in hand, she turned to the side and bent her knees, as her brothers had shown her. They'd given her a light sword so she could hold it with one hand, meaning she need not face her opponent fully and could make herself a smaller target.

An approving smile lit Conan's face. Her pulse raced in response. Damn, but he was handsome. She'd been in a man's bed before—as soon as she realized she'd never marry she decided she didn't particularly care what anyone else thought. Not that she was jumping from one to the next or flaunting any of her fun.

But it had been a *long* time. She hadn't thought of anything but the business and her sister since they opened the place. And that was four summers ago. No wonder she was swooning so easily.

He did her the decency of attacking instead of asking if she was ready or talking down to her, which she appreciated. He did hold back though. Alannah wasn't particularly skilled or experienced in swordplay, but she could tell he moved slower than he could, that he didn't rebound as quickly as he would have in a real fight. It irritated her, but even still she couldn't keep up.

"You won't break me," he grinned, taunting her. "Hit harder."

"These aren't practice swords," she reminded him, as though there were actually a chance she'd strike.

"If you make me bleed, I'll buy you a drink."

She snorted. That only meant he'd let her hit him.

"What?" he asked. "You don't believe me?"

"I don't *trust* you," she corrected, adjusting the grip on her sword. "You'll let me win."

He scoffed in what was clearly mock offense. "I would never." He held the pommel against his chest as though she'd struck him.

He was certainly dramatic enough to be a bard.

"How about this," he began, his voice softening. "Every time you win a bout, you can choose a prize. Every time I win, you cover one of my drinks for the night. Now I have incentive not to let you win," he grinned, his grey eyes sparkling with mischief.

Her stomach fluttered, but she ignored the rush. She'd never win if she didn't focus. "Every time I beat you, you have to answer a question," she decided, now invested in the game. "Truthfully."

"Is there another way?" he teased, taking up his stance.

Her eyes rolled as she matched him, attacking first and hoping to catch him by surprise. Steel met steel, and two moves later his blade stopped in front of her throat.

"Drink one." His voice was low, seductive.

It shouldn't have had any effect on her after that thorough defeat.

And yet, it did.

Again, he beat her.

And again.

Alannah lowered her sword to catch her breath, noting that Conan wasn't even breathing hard. "Looks like your drinks are on the house tonight," she panted. She needed to find a sparring partner or she'd never be able to adequately defend Emer should the need arise. "Go on," she sighed, "tell me how a woman has no business carrying a sword she can't wield."

"Is that what you believe I'm thinking?" he asked. "Has someone said that to you?"

Alannah laughed darkly. "You mean has someone *not* said that to me."

His jaw tightened.

Her heart reacted. Damnit. This man.

"That's the stupidest thing I've ever heard. You struggle because you need practice, not because you have tits," he said roughly, speaking as though she were one of his men and not some lady that needed gentle treatment.

"Do you still practice?" she asked. "Even though you're a bard?"

"Every day." He narrowed his eyes. "What do you mean 'still'?"

"I assumed that you lot were mercenaries with a change of heart or some such. Why else would a band of giants armed as warriors walk around as bards?"

"Giants?" he laughed.

"Compared with the rest of us, aye. Poor Emer has to look straight up at the lot of you, like she's talking to trees."

He chuckled from his belly, a sound that brought a smile her own face.

"Aye, we're all trained as warriors," he admitted, "but we don't like to speak of it."

She nodded her understanding. That made sense. And she knew all about leaving the past behind you. "Tell me how to beat you."

"Your technique isn't bad, just slow. The first thing you need is to practice, every single day, until you can fight with me and not be winded. Until every swing of your sword is so familiar you needn't think—only react." He took up his stance. "Again."

Alannah obeyed, knowing he did it to push her, to help her improve. This time she picked up her pace, throwing everything she had into every swing, every recovery.

He moved a little quicker, she noted with pleasure. She still hadn't even come close to landing a blow, but he'd had to work harder to block her.

"Ask me your question," he offered.

"But I didn't win. I don't need pity."

"Think of it more as motivation. You're exhausted, but you went again. Every time you pick that sword back up and fight me like your life depends on it, you win."

It made sense and it hurt her pride a little less, so Alannah decided to ask her question instead of arguing. "Why are you out here with me?"

"Because you intrigue me," he answered evenly. "Again."

He didn't give her time to weigh his answer, starting up the next bout before she could get control of her breathing again. Lord, this sword was heavy all of a sudden. As much as she wanted to earn his respect, she couldn't keep going. One move in, she lost her grip on her sword.

"My win," he grinned, picking up her sword, flipping it effortlessly, and handing it back to her. "But you've already covered all my drinks, so I'll play the question game." He paused, looking to her for consent.

She nodded, her heart hammering.

"Why are you resisting me?" He took a step toward her. "Are you really not interested?"

Alannah swallowed, her mouth going dry in spite of the damp that clung to the air. "No," her voice cracked. "I just doubt that you are."

"Why?" His dark brows knitted.

"Most men chase my sister. I'm not the prize."

His jaw tightened again, as it had earlier. Lord help her, she wanted to brush her fingers on it. "They don't chase her because she's the prize," he whispered. "They chase her because you're unattainable. They're outmatched, and they know it."

She could hardly breathe, but this time it had naught to do with swords. "And yet, here you are. Chasing."

His hand cupped the side of her face, rough and warm, as his eyes devoured her. "I'm not most men."

CHAPTER EIGHT

HIS THUMB RAN along the bottom of her cheek as he fought his self-control. He needed to make certain she understood what he was suggesting before he went any further.

"I'm not looking to court anyone," she told him softly, like she could read his mind.

"What are you looking for?"

Her eyes fell to his lips. "Just a little fun."

"How about a lot of fun for just a little while?" he offered. "We're only staying for a few weeks."

"Who says I need a few weeks of fun?" Her eyes darkened, raising to look up at him from beneath hooded lids. "How about one night of fun?"

That was all he needed to hear. The last thing he wanted was to start up a reputation like his brother had—the sort of man who beds his way across the island. He had no interest in leaving a string of broken hearts in his wake. But he wasn't going to live like a monk, either.

Without another thought, Conan gave into the desire he'd had since the moment they arrived. His lips came down on hers hungrily.

Her soft, sweet mouth opened to him, her tongue inviting him to delve deeper.

He happily obliged. The kiss was a frenzy of lust, a celebration of letting go. She tasted like temptation incarnate.

Dropping her sword, Alannah fisted his tunic and led him to

one of the small guest roundhouses. She shut the door behind them, drenching the room in darkness.

Conan blinked, but his vision never cleared. There was no light at all in the little room. He sensed her in front of him, though, and reached for her until his hands found her waist.

"I'm disappointed I don't get to see those muscles," she pouted. Her fingers danced over his chest, emphasizing her statement.

"Perhaps we'll have to make it two nights of fun," he whispered, moving them both to the cot he'd seen behind him before the door shut.

Her teeth scraped his bottom lip, sending a shiver through him. "Just one night. I can't afford a distraction as pretty as you."

A low rumble escaped him. He couldn't have said it better himself. "Then we'd better make it count."

With no light whatsoever, Conan relied entirely on his other senses, running his hands along her body, using his mouth to taste every inch of her. Her breasts filled his palms, and he would have given anything in that moment to actually see them. Instead, he used his tongue to tease the nipples until he felt them harden, until Alannah's soft moans grew ravenous.

"Conan," she begged, reaching for his hard length and guiding it toward her.

Every muscle in his body went taut as he entered her. She felt exquisite—velvety and wet and warm. He moved slowly at first, doing his best to torment them both.

But Alannah spurred him on, lifting her hips in a movement that drove him wild, shattering what little control he'd had in the first place.

Slipping his hand between them, Conan helped her spiral toward her own fulfillment.

The pressure that had built to the point of agony in the base of his spine finally gave way to his own release. He held still, listening to her heavy breaths slow and wondering if he really could keep his promise of only one night.

Because already he found himself wanting more of Alannah.

WHEN HE WOKE the next morn, Alannah was gone, the sun was up, and Conan had no regrets whatsoever. He couldn't savor the satisfaction of a night well spent for long, though, as Illadan would be after him if he kept them from getting their mission underway. They may have bought the room for a month, but that was a worst-case scenario. If things went well, they may only stay a sennight or less.

She was nowhere to be found in the main hall where they'd dined last night. Emer swept the floor while the other Fianna broke their fast at the corner table near the door.

Based on the absurd looks they gave him, Conan knew they only kept their mouths shut out of respect to Emer. He was, for all intents and purposes, the only true stag left among the eight of them now.

First Finn had married Dallan's sister, Eva, while Illadan was busy romancing Finn's sister, Ethlinn. Then Dallan had stumbled upon his first love and somehow won her over. Conan's younger brother, Diarmid, had stolen the King of Dyflin's intended bride. That he'd stolen another man's wife hadn't surprised Conan one bit. That the woman was willing had shocked him to no end. Even Conan's elder brother Cormac had charmed a woman to wife, an Ostman princess, no less.

Ardál had no wife, but he'd also shown no interest whatsoever in taking lovers, at least as far as Conan had observed. The man was a complete mystery, keeping even more to himself than Cormac.

And Broccan would never marry again. He never spoke of the wife and daughter he'd lost, but Conan knew it had broken him, changed him. He'd never been the same man after the fire. And he'd made it more than clear that he'd never take another wife.

One by one, they'd fallen prey to their hearts, which meant they had but one target to get in all of their obnoxious jests.

They finished eating without much conversation. Dallan looked barely conscious, and Conan knew his head must ache something fierce even though he didn't complain. When they were well out of earshot of The Hart's Rest, Illadan rounded on Conan.

"You cannot keep bedding her." He spoke under his breath, keeping the conversation quiet.

"I don't intend to," Conan assured him. Alannah herself had insisted it was for one night only, though he knew he'd be sorely tempted to see her again.

"Good," Illadan clipped. "Because if you bed her every night except the ones where we go to the bridge, she'll realize what we're up to. She has a sharp mind and an observant eye."

He was right. Conan nodded his understanding, grateful that at least someone had kept their head last night. "She thinks we're retired mercenaries," he told them all.

"Is that what you told her?" Finn asked from behind him.

"No, she decided it was the only reasonable explanation for a group of bards being so heavily armed and giant."

"Giant?" Dallan grinned.

"Her word."

"And you agreed to it?" Illadan pressed, his mind flying behind narrowed eyes.

"I did. I told her we didn't like to speak of it." Though he'd answered her truthfully, he hadn't loved the lie of omission. But his loyalty was to the Fianna. Unlike his younger brother, Conan wasn't about to risk a mission over a woman, no matter how beautiful.

THEY SPENT THE day out about the town, sure to stay clear of the king's residence to the north. Conan hadn't been in Ath Luain since he'd left at the age of seven to foster with Brian, so none of the townsfolk had much chance of recognizing him.

But he had seen his father, King Cahill of Connachta, a few months earlier. The king and his men would certainly recognize Conan on sight, along with the other Fianna. If they were discovered staying in town instead of accompanying Brian to the council meeting, their mission would be compromised.

The bridge proved a busier place than Conan imagined. Every time the Fianna neared it, someone was either crossing or within easy sight of it. They'd not have any hope of sneaking supplies out there during the day with this many people around.

"What day is it?" Finn asked.

"Thursday." Illadan had the answer before Conan could even process the question.

"We should try Sunday morning," Finn suggested. "The folk who aren't at church will be sleeping off their Saturday night."

The hint of a smile passed over Illadan's lips as he nodded in agreement.

Dallan smacked Finn's back affectionately. "Maybe you're not a total loss, after all."

"Your sister seems to think so," Finn taunted him.

"You did not just—"

Finn shrugged, walking back in the direction of The Hart's Rest and leaving Dallan grimacing.

Conan was enjoying not being at the wrong end of a joke for a change. "We should come back every day," he added. "Sunday may be best, but every town has a rhythm. Perhaps we'll have more than one option."

"Agreed." Illadan halted Finn. "Finn and Dallan, you find a reason to visit the western side of the bridge every day for the next sennight. Conan and Ardál, the eastern side. I'll see if I can learn anything from the locals. We still spar every morn. We can meet outside the town to the west."

"We can spar behind The Hart's Rest," Conan told him. "Alannah believes we still practice every day, so she won't think it odd."

"How did she fight?" Dallan turned to Conan, genuine curiosity in his tone.

"Fair enough for someone who doesn't make a living of it." She had the heart of a warrior, but the skill of a novice. With practice, she could be a worthy opponent to anyone.

"She needs a dagger to help her parry." Ardál's smooth voice slid into the conversation. "She'll be relying on her speed and will struggle with heavy blows."

"Then we'll make her one," Conan grinned, pleased with his idea. "The smithy is on the eastern side of the bridge, is he not?"

"Aye," Illadan agreed. "Do it."

Even though his involvement with Alannah was at its end, Conan's chest warmed at the idea of having a dagger made for her. It would serve her well, make her into an even better protector.

And she'd have something to remember him by when he was gone.

The way that thought tugged at his gut, Conan decided Illadan was absolutely right. Not only could it put them at risk of discovery, but spending more time with Alannah could also make leaving even more difficult.

They returned to The Hart's Rest in time for the evening meal. The gathering room smelled like heaven, warm spices and savory pork accompanying the familiar scent of peat smoke as they entered. Conan's pulse leapt when he spotted Alannah helping Emer deliver trenchers of stew to the busy room.

She still wore trews, sword hanging at her side, her dark hair in a messy plait. The memory of his hands threaded through her hair rose up, raising the temperature in the cozy room. Suddenly he was famished, his eyes fixed on her delicious hips as she walked back toward the kitchen.

Dallan's hand on his shoulder pulled him from his trance. "I don't know how you got her into your bed in the first place," his voice dripping with sarcasm, "staring like that. Did Diarmid teach you nothing?"

Conan shoved him. "Remind me again how many women have agreed to get into *your* bed?" He knew damn well it was only one.

"Unfair," Dallan countered. "She's the only one I asked. It's one by choice."

"Whatever you say." Conan patted him like a child before walking over to a table, satisfied in his small victory.

Emer may not have been the prize, but she certainly could cook. All five of the men devoured the stew, easily the best meal they'd had in months. And the cook at Cenn Cora was famously skilled. Alannah generally avoided their table, keeping busy helping her sister. Conan caught her looking his way once, but she never came over to speak with him.

They'd agreed it was for only one night, yet it stung his pride more than he liked that she seemed content to keep it that way. For his part, he'd happily have spent another with her if Illadan hadn't forbidden it. Deciding he wouldn't let the situation between them grow any more awkward, Conan waited until the guests had left for the night before pulling her aside in the far corner of the room. The rest of his companions retired to sleep. They had a long day tomorrow, starting with sparring at sunrise. With Conan's luck, Illadan would have them running laps around the town as he had in Dyflin.

That thought gave him another one—one that excited him more than it should.

"You ran away before I could thank you," he whispered, forcing himself to keep his eyes on her face.

"I had things to do." She managed to keep her face serious, but her eyes were just as playful as they'd been last night.

"That's good," he purred, "because I thought you were avoiding me."

"And I thought we agreed on one night."

"We did," he sighed, battling his rising desire. This was going to be a long month. "I had another proposition for you, actually."

The door flew open before he could tell her his idea.

The bastard from yesterday stormed into the room, looking just as furious as before.

"You have *got* to be kidding me," Conan growled. The man had clearly waited until he thought the women would be downstairs alone. Every muscle in Conan's body tensed, crying out to put him in his place.

"Get out." Alannah charged the man, a tempest unleashed. She didn't attack him, stopping an arm's length away, hands fisted on her hips.

As much as he wanted to run to her rescue, Alannah wasn't that kind of woman. She needed to deal with the fool on her own. His hands itched to interfere, his teeth grinding as he watched the exchange.

But he held back.

As far as he could tell, the man didn't realize Conan was there yet.

"If you don't stop stealing my business, you'll force me to take more drastic measures."

"If you don't find your own way to the door, I'll have to drag you there myself."

The man didn't back off. Instead, he moved closer. "I don't want to hit a woman."

Conan thought his teeth might crack.

But Alannah stood her ground, not giving an inch. "It sounds to me like you're looking for an excuse to do just that."

He'd give her two moves, then he was interfering. If she didn't get the upper hand in two moves, Conan was going to paint this bastard's face purple. Honestly, he might do it even if she did best him. He deserved no less for threatening two women over his own inability to conduct business.

The fight broke out as he'd expected. The man threw the first punch. Alannah dodged and missed her counterpunch. He landed his next one, propelling Alannah backward into a table.

Absolutely not.

Conan strode forward, more than prepared to ruin this man's night.

CHAPTER NINE

BLOOD TRICKLED FROM her nose, but she couldn't feel anything except fury. How could she have *ever* considered courting this man? Clearly, her judgment was not to be trusted.

Worse, even with all her brothers' training, Alannah knew she couldn't win this fight. For all her talk of protecting Emer, she couldn't do it when her sister needed her.

Emer.

The reminder of why she was prepared to take any number of blows brought her another wave of courage. Her sister was depending on her. Even if Conan came to aid her, she needed to keep going. One day soon, he wouldn't be here to back her up.

Oran stepped toward her, winding back for another blow.

She shoved off the table, preparing to block it.

She never got the chance.

Instead, the satisfying sound of Conan's fist connecting with Oran's face interrupted their brawl. He didn't give Oran a chance. The hits kept coming, one-two into his chest, another into his face, until he tumbled backwards, spitting out teeth.

Conan lifted Oran off the floor by his shirt, hauling him bodily to the door. "If you set foot in this building again, Alannah will kill you, and I'll make sure she doesn't owe the fine for it."

Good Lord. A storm of emotions stirred within her, so many she couldn't identify a single one as she watched the gorgeous giant defend her and respect her all in the same moment. He'd let her fight. He'd given her a chance to hold her own before stepping in.

He'd believed in her enough to wait.

"Alannah!" Emer shouted, hurrying to her from where she'd been washing dishes. "Are you alright?"

Alannah shook those silly, girlish thoughts from her mind. It was because she'd bedded him that she had a soft spot for him. Turning to Emer, she hurried to put her sister's worries at ease.

"I'm perfectly fine," she assured her. "Are you alright? I'm sorry I let him get inside."

"For heaven's sake, Alannah!" Emer tsked. "I'm not the one who took a fist to the face. Let me get you a cloth." She hustled back toward the kitchen.

After slamming the door on Oran and barring it, Conan rounded on her. The rage in his eyes dissolved into concern the moment he set eyes on her.

"Maybe I should have killed him." His nose flared in anger, his jaw clenching so tightly she could see the muscles working.

It sent a familiar warmth straight through her, the memory of a sensation she craved but could not give into. It would be foolish to get too attached to a man just passing through—even one so interesting as Conan.

"He's not worth the effort," she told him, the pain finally settling in her nose. "Did he break it?"

Conan's fingers gingerly ran the length of her nose and moved over her cheeks. "Luckily for him, he did not." His squared jaw ticked tellingly. "So when you said he came by occasionally, what you meant was he threatened you nearly every day?"

Alannah swallowed, testing her own sore jaw. "Something like that, aye."

"You should run with us tomorrow," he told her. "At sunrise we train, and you should, too."

"Run?"

"You'll get less winded for it." His voice fell on her like a caress, soft and tender as he inspected her nose further. "I think it should heal fine."

Swallowing the last shreds of her pride, Alannah sighed. "Thank you."

"You didn't need me." The corner of his mouth raised into a half-smile. "I just couldn't wait any longer. I meant what I told him," his tone turned serious. Deadly.

Alannah could see now how he'd been a mercenary once, perhaps not that long ago.

"If he comes back, use your sword. I'll make sure no trouble comes of it."

"How?" She wasn't certain she trusted him, but she did believe him. The idea of killing anyone, even Oran, didn't sit well with her. But if it came down to protecting Emer from him, she just might.

"I know people," was all the answer he offered. "I'll see you at sunrise."

He took his leave and Emer took his place, carefully washing the blood from Alannah's face.

"Does it hurt?" she asked. "It looks like it hurts."

Her face felt like that shattered pot from last night, in spite of Conan's reassurances. But she wasn't about to have Emer thinking she couldn't protect her. "Not at all."

Emer shook her head. "You're such a sweet liar."

"Emer, if he comes back, I need you to promise you'll run. Hide. Especially if I'm not here."

"Alannah," Emer protested.

"Promise." She wouldn't stop until she got her sister's word.

"I promise," she acquiesced finally.

Alannah let out a breath. At least if she failed to protect Emer, her sister would still have a chance of escape. Hopefully her brothers truly were on their way back as Glasny had said. With Oran's increased hostility she'd feel better having them here. Oran was a bully but he wasn't a fool. He'd wait until the bards left before trying anything again.

Once Emer finished her ministrations, Alannah retired to their shared room, exhausted. Laying there, staring at the ceiling, more memories of Conan flooded her sleepy thoughts. She'd been right about him twice over.

He'd been holding back when they sparred last night. She'd struggled to land a single blow and Conan could've killed Oran as an afterthought. That man was lethal.

And she'd been right that she could only spend one night with him. Her body heated in desperation for another, but Alannah knew it was for the best to keep her distance—as much as possible while sharing the inn with him, anyway. Alannah had been too distracted by Conan to pay attention to the door. If she'd been keeping watch as she always did, Oran wouldn't have entered at all.

Conan was a distraction she couldn't afford.

DECIDING TO STAY away from Conan was one thing, but physically doing so was another entirely. Alannah learned as much the following morn when she joined the men on their run. Aside from childhood games, Alannah had never run for the sake of running, and never for so long a time.

Brutal did not begin to cover it.

Gasping for breath and doing her best to hide it, Alannah pushed herself until her lungs burned and she was certain she would lose her breakfast. Somewhere northwest of Ath Luain, she had to lean against a tree to catch her breath.

"Head between your knees," Conan's voice advised.

She did as he instructed, doubling over and lowering her head. It helped. She took several long, slow breaths. Even though she managed to catch her breath, her heart still raced and her legs burned.

"I'll walk you back," he offered.

Alannah shook her head, straightening slowly. "I can keep going."

"Maybe you can," he allowed, "but you shouldn't. Join us again tomorrow and you'll make it further before you must stop."

"I'm not going to ruin your run for the next month," she told him. "I'll keep coming, but you don't need to walk me back."

"That's not optional." His tone brooked no argument. "Not after last night."

"Oran was after Emer, not me."

He narrowed his grey-blue eyes at her as they walked back the way they'd come. His gaze strayed from her face, roaming slowly, deliberately, over every inch of her. The way he devoured her made her fight to breathe for entirely different reasons. "Right, that's why he was attacking *you*. Because he's after Emer."

"He keeps trying to catch her on her own," Alannah explained, horrified at how much her lungs yet burned. No wonder she struggled to spar for any length of time. "She's so delicate and gentle, she'd never be able to defend herself. He keeps attacking me because I keep getting in his way."

"Why?"

"I told you, she can't defend herself."

He smiled. "No, I mean why is he going after her?"

"I think he realizes that without her there'd be no Hart's Rest. I couldn't do the things she does to run it, not without hiring help I can't afford."

"And he runs the other inn in Ath Luain?"

Alannah could as good as hear him trying to solve the problem, trying to work it out. "Aye. He opened it to try to run us out of business after I left him."

Conan stopped dead. "After you *what*?"

CHAPTER TEN

UNBELIEVABLE, THIS WOMAN. Could she truly not see the problem here?

"He courted me not long after we opened the inn, but I didn't like him once we spent time together. He got angry over it and opened his inn across the river to steal customers from us before they got further into town."

"And you somehow believe he's motivated by your sister?" Conan couldn't believe they were even having such a ridiculous conversation. For what felt the hundredth time that morn, he forced his gaze away from her heaving chest and the delicious imaginings that brought to mind. "If you were the one he wanted, I promise it's not your sister he now desires."

Alannah shrugged. "I think he started out trying to get back at me. But it's turned into an attack on the inn, and Emer is the heart of the inn."

"Or maybe he realizes the best way to hurt you is to hurt her." Either way, Conan would end this nonsense. He couldn't leave knowing a madman was after them. "Why does he keep accusing you of stealing his business?"

He wanted to kiss the smug grin that claimed her lips.

"When he opened his hostelry on the eastern shore, it was easy for him to stop travelers before they had to ford the river. And most folk don't want to get soaked right before they tuck in for the night. Our business suffered for it until the bridge went up.

"Before, even when I paid Glasny to recommend folk to The Hart's Rest, they often just stayed where they'd not need to cross at the ford that night. But now that there's an easy way to cross, I've made a few friends around town who don't mind telling people how great The Hart's Rest is in exchange for a small cut of our profit."

Conan's chest tightened every time she mentioned the bridge. If it had saved their business, then burning it would hurt them. It would hurt her.

He didn't like that thought one bit.

"Do a lot of people on the western shore feel that way as well?" he asked. "That the bridge has made things easier?"

She nodded emphatically. "Everyone I've spoken with, including folk who live in the farms on the west of town. It's easier for them to head inland to markets."

Damn. That was not what he wanted to hear at all. "Then it's a good thing that bridge was built," was all he could manage, and he felt like an arse for saying it even as he was plotting to burn it down.

He'd been planning to work with her on her fist fighting, but the knot forming in his gut told him that was a dangerous game to start playing. Already guilt threatened his resolve. He was here to burn down that bridge and then get out of town. He doubted he'd ever come back, either.

Illadan was right—he needed to stay away from Alannah.

ALANNAH LINGERED FOR just a few moments. Not because she thought she should stay, but because she didn't want to go. When Conan nodded and turned away, she took that as her sign to do the same. And the first order of business following that run was a wash. She hadn't been covered in so much sweat since she built the last guest cottage. Wandering into the common room of The

Hart's Rest, Alannah found Emer sweeping out the sleeping compartments along the outside of the room, her ochre skirts swishing in time with the broom.

"I'm going down to the river to wash," she told her sister. "Want to keep me company?" Alannah did want Emer's company, of course. She loved her sister dearly. But she also didn't like the idea of leaving her here alone right after Oran's most recent attack. He'd been far more violent of late.

Concerningly so.

Emer's smile faltered for but a moment before returning, brighter than ever. "Of course! Let me grab some bedding to clean."

"You're going to swim, too, right?" They always swam together. Emer loved the water as much as Alannah, and it was far more fun to go with one another.

Emer hesitated. "I've already done so."

Alannah narrowed her eyes. Emer never refused to swim. "Are you alright?"

"Of course, of course," her sister hurried, pulling a basket of linens from the floor and hoisting it onto her hip. "I just need to get these cleaned."

Something wasn't right, but Alannah couldn't decide what it might be. Perhaps Emer was more tired than usual after Oran came by twice in the past two days. When they got to the river, no doubt she'd change her mind and join in the fun.

Alannah carried a second basket of linens, leading the way down the path and into Ath Luain. It was nearing midday, and the sun was out for the first time in days, blazing above and beckoning everyone outside to enjoy the beautiful weather. Including the bards, it would seem.

Alannah and Emer found the men scattered about town. Dallan and Finn wandered near the market square, perusing the myriad wares. Conan and Ardál stepped onto the bridge, heading to the eastern shore. When they reached the grassy river bank, they found Illadan sitting on the bridge fishing. He was too far out to call out to, probably near halfway across the wide causeway. Alannah wasn't even certain whether he saw them, for he made no motion to indicate that he had.

Moving to their usual swimming spot, protected enough to keep them out of easy sight of the entire village, Alannah stripped down and laid out her clothes, wading into the brisk water. No one else was around, which surprised her given the warm, sunny day. It was perfect for a swim.

Smiling and turning her face up to the sun, she danced her fingers over the water, rippling it around her. The river had warmed considerably in just the past two days.

"You should get in," she called to Emer. "It feels wonderful."

On the shore, Emer sat dunking a bed sheet. "I should get these washed."

"I'll help you." Alannah swam over, running her hands across her arms and body to get the sweat and grime off. Grabbing the next sheet, she got to work.

Between the two of them, the washing was done in no time. Emer stayed oddly quiet as they worked, raising Alannah's suspicions even more. Folding the last sheet and plopping it into the basket to carry home and hang out, Alannah turned back to her sister. "Alright, the wash is done. Now you can get in and enjoy yourself," she declared.

"I don't know if I feel like swimming today."

"You always feel like swimming," Alannah countered, her brow creasing. "You love swimming."

Emer shrugged, moving her legs out from under her as though she intended to leave already.

Alannah's hand shot out, resting on her sister's knee. "Emer, what's going on? You're not swimming. You're hardly speaking. What's wrong?"

A heavy sigh escaped Emer's rosy lips. "I will swim, but only if you swear not to overreact."

Alannah froze, a shiver of foreboding running down her spine. "Overreact to *what?*"

"Promise," Emer pressed.

Alannah didn't like the desperation in her sister's voice. "I promise."

Emer took off her dress, laying it on dry grass. When her arm slipped out of her chemise, Alannah marched straight out of the water, taking her sister's hand and pulling her arm closer.

It was covered in bruises.

Fingerprint-shaped bruises.

Oran. It had to have happened the day the bards came, when Alannah thought she'd arrived just in time to get him out before he hurt Emer. Apparently, she hadn't quite made it.

Her head buzzed as ice crystallized in her veins. "I'm going to kill him."

"No!" Emer squealed, pulling her chemise back on. "See, this is exactly what I was worried about. You're going to get *yourself* killed. I'm just fine."

"You're not fine!" Alannah grabbed her trews, struggling to pull them on over her wet legs. "And I warned him."

"You promised not to overreact."

Alannah tugged her léine over her head, giving her loose hair a good swish to get it out of the way. "I'm not overreacting. I'm reacting appropriately. Stay here."

Ignoring Emer's continued protests, Alannah took off toward the causeway.

And vengeance.

CHAPTER ELEVEN

THE BLACKSMITH'S WORKSHOP was built of stone on the far eastern edge of Ath Luain, placed far from any other buildings to prevent the spread of fire. The packed earth floor was littered with tools that Conan didn't know the first thing about. A fire-filled forge took up the back left corner of the square cottage. On the right side of the room, lit by a window and the door, two anvils sat waiting, hammers perched atop each.

Conan tested the weight of the example dagger the smith had handed him. "What'll it cost to have the handle laid with gold filigree?"

"An extra three ounces of silver." The smith's thick, grey beard moved as he rumbled his reply. "And it'll add two days' time."

"That's no trouble." In fact, it was perfect. They needed the dagger to be complex enough that it took the better part of a sennight, giving them several days of excuses to cross the causeway and wander the eastern shore.

Conan handed the dagger back to the smith, along with the first two ounces of silver—a full forty silver pennies, half of the cost of the elaborate dagger. Before he could ask the smith when they could expect it, Emer tumbled through the open door behind them in her underdress, wide-eyed.

"Conan!" She leaned against the door frame, catching her breath. "Alannah's going after Oran! She went to his hostelry. You've got to stop her."

Swearing under his breath, Conan bolted past Emer. While he didn't disagree that Oran deserved to have his arse handed to him, Alannah had no business attempting that alone. Unprovoked, he could try to exact a fine from her—if he didn't beat her, that was. Alannah was fierce, but untrained. Without more practice, she'd not be able to win against Oran.

Luckily, Oran's guesting house was a few buildings away, just south of the smithy. He heard shouting the moment he stepped out into the glaring sun. The door to the large, wooden building was already open, the cries from within escalating to screams as he stepped inside.

And came to a full, sudden stop.

Two men who looked as though they had piles of rocks where their minds ought to be held a struggling Alannah back by her arms.

And his brothers held back Oran.

Conan's pulse raced so fast that he thought his heart would give out. Glancing about the room, he noted that it wasn't just Cormac and Diarmid. Broccan and Brian stood inside the common room as well, no doubt investigating the commotion.

God's bones they must've been passing through when Alannah came in here. At least it hadn't been Teague or his father. But still, this was a far more delicate situation than he'd expected. If Alannah discovered that he knew any of them, their ruse would be compromised, along with the mission.

Diarmid noticed Conan first, his blue eyes widening beneath dark brows. He nudged Cormac, who turned a similarly shocked expression on Conan. Broccan picked up on the change in the room, as did Brian, who both turned to watch Conan approach. Brian's face was unreadable. Broccan's was furious, though that likely had little to do with Conan. Broccan seemed more angry than not these days.

"Apologies for the interruption," Conan began, stepping in between the squirming Alannah and a scowling Oran. "Alannah, Emer sent me to make sure you didn't get yourself killed."

"You know this woman?" Brian demanded.

"I do." Conan turned toward his king. "My friends and I have been staying at her guesting house while we perform in the area."

"You're—what—bards, then?" Broccan demanded, knowing full well the ruse they'd planned.

Conan nodded once. "We are. And if it's all the same to you, I'd like to get my gracious host back to her hostelry."

"I'm not leaving until he's dead!" Alannah shouted unhelpfully.

"I'm afraid there won't be any killing today, young lady," Brian chuckled. At least he found this all amusing. "What manner of dispute do you have with this man, to attack him in his own home?"

"He attacked my sister!" She groaned in frustration when the men yanked her further from Oran. "She's covered in bruises!"

Conan's stomach dropped. "What?" He drew his sword, stepping toward Oran.

"Ah." Brian called, the sound clearly intended to halt Conan.

Reluctantly, he turned toward the king. "I saw the attack," Conan told him. "What she says is true."

"Ignore that old man and help me exact justice," Alannah demanded.

Out of the corner of his eye, Conan caught Diarmid's grin at Alannah's choice of words.

"Watch how you speak to the King of Mumhain, girl." Broccan's threat held more malice than Conan liked.

Alannah froze, her gaze sliding from Oran to Brian. "You're Brian Bóruma mac Cennétig?"

Brian crossed his arms and stepped into the fray. "I am."

"We had no idea," Conan apologized.

The corner of Brian's bearded mouth lifted in amusement. "Of course not. How could you?" He gave Alannah his full attention now. "I'm afraid that, regardless of his attack on your sister, I still cannot allow you to slay him. However, you are entitled to the full payment of the fine on her behalf. She had bruising, you say? For God's sake, let the woman go."

Alannah and Oran were both released. Before she could make any rash decisions, Conan walked right up to her and took her hand in his, giving it a squeeze.

"Yes, lord," Alannah replied, squaring off with the king. "And he broke into our home, I believe with intent to do more than just that."

"Lies!" Oran spat, storming toward her.

Conan stepped in the way. Cormac and Diarmid took hold of Oran's arms again.

"All she ever does is slander me!"

This time, Brian turned to Conan. "Is that true?"

"It is not, lord," Conan replied honestly. Alannah had told him she paid for folk to praise her business, not slander his. "He doesn't have the right of it."

"You lying son of a—"

"That's quite enough from you," Brian interrupted. "You will pay the victimized woman's family three ounces of silver. If there is a repeat offense, the fine will triple."

"You're not king here!" Oran argued. "It's Cahill's laws we follow, not yours."

Brian didn't look the least flustered by Oran's continued outbursts. "He's just down the way if you'd prefer I fetch him. I doubt he'll be pleased at being disturbed over something I've already handled, though."

Oran roared in agitation, but didn't argue further.

"Good," Brian announced. "Now that that's settled, let's be on our way." He turned a sharp eye on Conan. "Can I trust you to see the lady back home once she's collected her payment?"

"Yes, lord," Conan assured him.

"I don't have the coin now," Oran muttered.

Brian tsked. "Then you will give her your sword."

Conan took great pleasure in watching Oran take off his sword belt and drop it on the ground, like a child throwing a tantrum over sweets. Alannah retrieved it, pinning Oran with a menacing glare. If the king hadn't been standing there with his warriors, Conan had no doubt she'd have pulled it on him.

Without another word, Brian strode out of the guesting house, Broccan, Cormac, and Diarmid right behind him.

Conan sighed in relief a moment too soon.

"Cahill!" He heard Brian call loudly. "We were just on our way to your home."

He heard his father's voice just beyond the doorway, a chill coursing through him. It was a sound he'd hoped never to hear again.

"This isn't finished," Oran growled, taking a step toward Alannah.

Conan didn't have time for this nonsense. He couldn't risk his father catching him. Taking Alannah's hand, he headed to the back door—as far as he could get from the bastard who'd sired him.

CHAPTER TWELVE

"WHERE ARE YOU going?" Alannah demanded, pulling on Conan's arm to stop him. "We should go tell Cahill of Oran's constant attacks while we can get the king's ear."

Conan frowned. "We should go check on your sister," he countered. "She was worried sick over you and only partly dressed."

"We were at the river to swim," she explained. "She must've chased right after me to get you."

"Thank goodness she did." He started walking again, looking around the back corner of the building before stepping around it. Though the wall of the hostelry was straight, boxes of stores were piled against it, and barrels stuck out from both corners. He paused, holding still and listening.

Why was he behaving so oddly? First Emer, now Conan. What was going on today? "Conan?"

Instead of walking all the way to the front of the building where it met the road, Conan turned toward the cooper's workshop, pulling Alannah behind him.

"Conan!" she demanded when he didn't offer any explanation.

The sound of hoofbeats echoed from the front of Oran's guesting house. Conan picked up his pace, yanking her behind the cooper's back wall between two stacks of boxes. He pressed her against the wall, his body pinning hers in place so that they were hidden from view.

"Conan," she hissed quietly. "What is going on?"

His throat bobbed. "I've crossed paths with the King of Connachta before," he whispered. "He would not be pleased to see me again, nor I him."

Alannah stiffened. "Would he be upset to learn that I'm hosting you?"

"No, no," Conan hurried. "He'd not be cross with you over it. Only me."

She narrowed her eyes skeptically, but held her tongue. If he'd been a mercenary in the past, it was certainly possible they'd met that way. Still, the more Alannah learned of Conan, the less she felt she knew about him.

The hoofbeats moved toward them down the road, headed in the direction of the causeway. Conan raised an arm, squeezing even closer and leaning his head right beside hers.

Alannah's heart hammered. He was so close. His warm, hard body pressed on hers and his intoxicating scent surrounded her, reminding her of all the things she wanted but couldn't have. His hands back on her. His lips claiming hers again. His cock deep inside her.

Damnit. Alannah swallowed against the dryness in her mouth. But when she sensed Conan's eyes on her, she made the mistake of turning her head.

His blue-grey eyes softened, his gaze darkening as it caressed her face and fell to her chest.

Her breath caught when his hand fell to her waist, his thumb circling the skin just beneath the hem of her tunic. She shouldn't let him touch her again. But instead of pushing him away, she melted against the wall behind her, slowly raking her hands over the thick muscles on his chest, savoring the feel of them beneath her fingertips.

He leaned down, his lips a breath away from her neck.

Her skin turned to gooseflesh in anticipation.

Then he pulled away. "Alannah," he whispered, his voice gravelly and broken, "I'm leaving in less than a fortnight." His forehead fell against hers, smooth and warm and comforting.

"I know," she whispered back, uncertain how she found her voice amidst the desire running rampant through her. "One night only."

His rough hand, covered in calluses from years of wielding his sword, rose to cup her face. "One night only."

He backed away, releasing her from the crush of his body, and walked beside her in silence back to The Hart's Rest.

THE REST OF that week was spent avoiding Alannah and scouting the bridge. He had come far too close to kissing that temptress, even with the threat of discovery looming so near. He'd bedded her, aye, but that was before they'd spent any amount of time together. Getting to know a person was much different than sharing their bed. The more time they spent together, the more dangerous a kiss would become, the more meaning it would hold. And Conan was leaving soon—he couldn't afford to have his resolve waver. If he got any closer to Alannah, he had no doubt whatsoever that it would.

They continued playing to perpetuate their ruse as bards. Conan and Ardál checked in with the blacksmith every afternoon. Illadan took to fishing off the bridge every afternoon—perhaps the most ridiculous cover Conan could've imagined for their leader. Illadan looked even less like a fisherman than he did a bard.

Between their efforts, they'd managed to stuff kindling and hide oil on either end of the bridge and beneath it, in case they needed more fuel.

Brian's party had come and gone, riding north as planned along with the other kings.

Which meant it was time.

The plan was simple. Conan and Ardál would keep watch

while Dallan, Finn, and Illadan set the bridge afire. The trick would be getting it to burn fast and hot so that once folk noticed they couldn't put it out in time to save it.

There was only one rule: don't be seen. They all wore hooded cloaks, just in case.

"We need this to work," Illadan reminded them as they huddled under the bridge in the early hours of the morning. The moon neared the horizon, but the sun wouldn't appear for hours yet. Even folk who'd stayed out late or got up early would be sound asleep right now. "We don't have many more supplies. If this goes wrong, we'll be stuck here until we can procure more and try again."

They all nodded their understanding. As pleasant as the hostelry was, none of them wanted to stay longer than needed. Finn's wife was heavy with child. Illadan had left his new baby to come on this mission. Everyone had a reason to make sure this worked.

And Conan couldn't take another agonizing day of pretending he wasn't still interested in Alannah.

Conan took up the post on the western side, Ardál the eastern. He didn't hear a sound as he gazed out into the sleeping streets of Ath Luain, and he didn't dare a glance behind him. With his luck, the moment he turned his head, someone would stumble into sight.

The smell of burning oil filled his nostrils, a faint flicker of light cast dancing shadows at his feet.

The shadows grew longer. Heat billowed against his back.

But the men still hadn't called out that they'd finished.

Conan shifted his weight, narrowing his eyes at a cluster of shadows along the side of a building at the edge of the nearest road. They were taking too long. He didn't know how long it had been, but he knew it shouldn't take so long to light wood afire. The shadows moved again, a cat emerging to stretch languidly.

Conan exhaled slowly. They needed to get out of here before they drew attention.

Lights appeared in town. Someone woke. Then all hell broke loose.

"Fire!" Shouts rose up, a symphony of panic, first from the western shore, then the eastern.

Conan whistled to the men, signaling they needed to leave, before ducking under the bridge. Four splashes told him they followed. They swam south to the ford, sheltered enough from sight between the embankments and the cover of night to sneak away unseen.

Soaking wet and freezing, the five Fianna warriors flopped like fish onto the shore once they were clear of Ath Luain.

"What happened?" Conan demanded.

"It wouldn't light," Dallan grumbled. "They coated it."

"It lit," Illadan corrected, entirely too composed. "It didn't spread as it should. We'll need to start fires every foot or so to burn through the coating."

"We need twice as many materials as we had, and we used them all," Finn sighed.

Conan shook his head. "We need a new plan."

"We'll circle around Ath Luain, dry off, and sneak into our room. Sleep if you can, but we still run at sunrise. Tomorrow afternoon we'll come up with a new plan."

They made it all the way to The Hart's Rest before the rest of their plan fell apart. Dried and exhausted, Conan stepped around the corner.

And straight into Alannah.

CHAPTER THIRTEEN

A LANNAH HOPPED BACK in surprise, squinting to be certain it wasn't Oran who'd come to take advantage of the chaos. When she realized it was Conan, her shoulders lightened in relief.

"Are you alright?" he asked, glancing around with concern. "We heard shouting."

"There's a fire," she explained, scrambling to grab the nearest bucket and pointing toward the blaze that towered above Ath Luain.

Conan nodded, calling to the rest of the bards to get buckets.

They ran together toward the spire of flame. Fires were no small matter in a town of wood and thatch. Everyone came out to keep it from spreading.

As they neared the heart of the commotion, Alannah's gut sank in realization.

The bridge was burning.

Grateful that she'd been building her stamina over the past sennight with the oddly fit bards, Alannah pushed herself even harder. Her lungs burned as she took up a position running empty buckets back to be filled. Conan took a spot filling buckets.

Luckily, they'd caught the fire early. If it had gone much longer, it would've rendered the bridge unsafe. Though it was blackened and charred like a battle-scarred warrior, it remained intact. The flames hadn't spread quickly, though that served as little consolation to Alannah.

She was no fool—she knew *precisely* who'd done this.

Oran.

He'd almost out and admitted it the night he attacked her. *Don't make me take more drastic measures.* Fury ignited like tinder as Alannah thought of him trying to burn the bridge just to ruin her business.

But she wasn't without her own resources. A plan formed, a damned good one, and Alannah's spirits lifted. She may not have been there to stop Oran tonight.

But next time, she would be.

As folk meandered back home, Alannah found Conan—knee-deep in the river, sleeves rolled up to reveal muscled forearms that brought back delicious memories. Swallowing hard, she pushed all thoughts of those hands on her to the back of her mind.

"Thank you for helping," she began, standing on the shore, trying not to gawk as he walked out of the water.

"Of course." He glanced back at the bridge. "It looks like it'll be okay."

"I know that this week has been awkward," she grimaced, "but I have a favor to ask."

His eyes narrowed, his gaze wary.

"I want you to keep practicing with me. I want to be able to fight."

He strode over to her. "I don't want to hurt you when I leave."

Butterflies took control of her stomach. "I was planning on practicing in the yard, not my bed." If only.

"And you think that will work? Spending all day together and then staying apart all night?"

The husky tone in his voice told her exactly what he thought, but it didn't matter. This wasn't about her love life.

It was about her family. And family was everything.

"I do."

"Then I'll see you at sunrise."

ALANNAH DIDN'T RETURN to bed. Instead she stayed up and helped Emer fix breakfast for their guests. The pilgrims had long since moved on, but they had a small family staying on their way to visit relatives. With two young girls and two older boys, Alannah couldn't stop thinking of her brothers.

Ossian and Osgar had been gone for so long. There wasn't a day she didn't worry over them. Had they seen many battles? Were they injured? Would they come home?

"They're so sweet, aren't they?" Emer smiled at the children, following their parents over to a table. She piled some apple tarts onto a plate.

Alannah knew exactly where those were headed. "You'll have your own one day."

Emer shrugged her delicate shoulders, grabbing as many plates and trenchers as she could balance. "Perhaps. You always joke that you're so old, but I'm only four years younger than you. Maybe that's not the life we were meant for."

The wistful look in her sister's eyes told a different story, but Alannah kept her mouth shut. She watched Emer dote on the children, passing them each a sweet along with their breakfast. Her sister was such a special person. The world needed more Emers.

"Are you up for running again?"

Alannah turned to find Finn smiling as he watched the wholesome scene unfolding in the common room. "Of course. And I'm training with you, too."

He glanced at her, raising a brow. "Is that so?"

"I asked Conan to help me. After that fight with Oran and now the bridge getting attacked," she swallowed. "I need to be able to protect her."

Finn tensed visibly. "Believe me, I understand that notion all too well."

That piqued Alannah's interest. "You speak as though from experience."

"My sister was hunted by a man once. If not for Illadan, she'd be dead." All the light had left his blue eyes, his face hardened. "If Conan can't teach you, I will." With that, he pushed away from the door and took his usual seat at the corner table.

She knew the moment Conan entered the room. It felt like all the air disappeared and she was fighting to breathe. The grin on his face when he spotted her didn't help matters, and neither did the intense run that followed.

This time, she made it through half the route before she had to stop. Not great, but better. As he did every time she stopped, Conan appeared at her side, waiting patiently as her body remembered how to breathe.

"How far can you run?" she asked, finally able to stand straight without gasping.

That same grin answered her question, the one that felt like it was just for her. "Farther than you."

She shoved him as hard as she could.

He didn't even stumble.

"I mean it."

"So do I," he laughed. "I've never measured it. I run as far as Illadan makes me run. When we stayed in Dyflin we ran around the entire city, so it must've been a few miles. I can run farther, but I avoid it if I can."

"You've been to Dyflin?" Alannah had always wondered what a town run by the invaders would be like. "Was it dangerous?"

"No, they were very welcoming. Of course, when you offer entertainment wherever you go, folk tend not to mind you visiting."

"Is Dyflin like Luimneach?" She couldn't stop herself. Curiosity got the better of her sense. Both towns had a large population of the northern invaders settled there, but Ath Luain was equally far from both places.

"Aye. Many houses are built in the style of their people, many folk speak the language and follow the rules and customs of the Ostmen, but not all." He looked over at her as they walked. "If you want to learn of the Ostmen, you need only ask Finn. His father is one."

"Well, that explains why *he's* so tall," she laughed, "but what of the rest of you?"

Conan caught her gaze, pausing to bite his bottom lip. "Just lucky, I guess," he drawled, his voice rough.

Alannah's stomach flipped. He couldn't have meant her. They weren't courting. It had only been the one night, and that certainly wasn't what he meant. Lord, she was turning into a proper fool over him.

Desperate for a change of subject, she returned to Finn. "That means Illadan is married to an Ostwoman," she thought aloud, "if he wed Finn's sister."

"Half of one, aye. But my brother married a woman from Dyflin with hair so red it looks like fire."

"You have a brother?"

They'd nearly reached The Hart's Rest, but Alannah didn't want the conversation to end. It enchanted her, learning about Conan's life and his friends. She'd only just realized she knew nothing of his family.

"I have three brothers and one sister," he sighed.

"Are you not close to them?"

"Two of my brothers I see quite often, my sister a few times a year. My eldest brother—" he halted mid-speech, tightening his face in obvious frustration. "I cannot forgive what he did."

"I'm sorry." Instinctively, she placed a hand on his arm, hot as a forge beneath her fingers. She couldn't imagine what that would be like, but she knew it would be hard. Her brothers and Emer were her entire world. Family was everything.

They stopped in the yard behind the barn, where they'd sparred before. Thankfully it hadn't rained in a few days, so the mud had turned into packed dirt once again.

"I'll go fetch my sword." She moved to walk past Conan.

He held an arm out, catching her so she couldn't pass. "No sword today."

She should move. Back away. Push forward. She should do

anything except stand there enjoying the press of his hand against her hip.

His eyes darkened, storm clouds rolling through the blue-grey irises. "You need to know how to throw a punch."

Her hand absently lifted to her nose, where the bruises had only just finished healing.

Conan nodded, his hazy eyes devouring her. "Your sword didn't do you any good, and you know enough to defend yourself with it. You need to know how to defend yourself without it."

His hand squeezed her hip, Alannah's desire coming to life at his touch. She didn't know what was happening, only that she didn't want it to stop. Beyond that, her thoughts fell away like leaves in the autumn.

The approach of footsteps broke the spell. His hand fell from her body. They each took a step back. The hunger in his eyes lingered until the rest of the men joined them.

Still, Alannah felt the pull toward him, her hip warm where his hand had been.

Where she wished it still were.

Everything in her screamed that it was reckless to want anything more with this man. But in that moment, she realized that she did.

CHAPTER FOURTEEN

H E COULDN'T TAKE the way she looked at him. He knew that look all too well—it was the one he hadn't been able to resist the night they arrived in Ath Luain.

"I'm going to need you to punch me," he managed.

It took her several seconds to process his words. Then she was back, feisty as ever.

"I thought you'd never ask," she grinned, taking up the stance she used with her sword and balling her fists.

"Wait, you're teaching her to fist fight?" Dallan asked, squaring up against Finn. "What happened to her sword?"

"When Oran attacked me the other night, it was a fistfight," she answered.

Dallan and Finn both turned to Conan. He hadn't told them about it. He wasn't trying to be secretive, it just hadn't felt like his story to tell.

"You didn't notice the giant bruise on her face?"

"Of course I did," Dallan scoffed. "I'm just too much of a gentleman to comment on it, obviously."

"Well, if Conan hadn't been there, bruises on my face would've been the least of my problems."

Finn lowered his sword, focused entirely on them now. "Wait. How was Conan there? Wasn't this the day we arrived?"

"It was the next night," Conan replied. "After you went to bed Oran broke through the front door. Alannah handled it more or less on her own."

She smacked his shoulder, rolling her eyes. "They know perfectly well I couldn't have won that fight."

"Actually, based on the situation when we arrived, I assumed you could best him handily," Dallan told her.

"She'll never best anyone if you lot don't start practicing," Illadan bellowed, blocking a blow from Ardál.

Conan returned his focus to the beauty in front of him. He lifted his hand, palm out, creating a target for her. "Hit me."

THEY SPARRED UNTIL midday. By then Alannah had mastered how to properly form a fist and land a right hook, but they had a long way to go before she'd be winning any bouts. After that, she had to hurry off to run errands in town for the inn.

The Fianna washed in a nearby creek, taking the opportunity to discuss their next strategy for destroying the bridge.

"What if we break it instead of burning it?" Dallan suggested.

Conan shot him a look. "Do you honestly think that would be faster? Or draw less attention?"

"Well it can't be worse than not working," he grumbled.

"We could get caught," Illadan reminded him. "Destroying the bridge doesn't matter if Cahill realizes Brian was behind it."

Conan gritted his teeth at the mention of his father. He understood the value of political alliances, of not exacting vengeance at every slight. But he couldn't understand how Brian let his father live, let alone how he met with him on friendly terms.

"Did they coat the bottom?" he asked.

As one, the Fianna turned their attention on him. It took only moments for each of them in turn to realize what he suggested.

"Even if they did," Illadan thought aloud, "it would be far easier to scrape the bottom than the top. That's brilliant, Conan."

"It provides cover, is fairly easy to access, and isn't close enough to the water to put out the fire." Dallan nodded in approval. "I think it might just work."

"We can plant tinder over several days or even weeks," Finn added, grinning. "No one will notice it tucked between the bottom braces."

"That's the new plan," Illadan announced. "We'll need to wait a few days before we start sneaking out to the bridge. No doubt the town will be on their guard. In the meantime, we spend the afternoons collecting tinder in the woods and stacking it to dry."

They decided on the details as they dressed and walked back to The Hart's Rest. It was a good plan. Burning the causeway was the entire reason they'd come to Ath Luain. And yet, with every step he took toward the guesting house, guilt weighed heavier on Conan. It was a damned good thing he wasn't continuing his involvement with Alannah because, try as he might, he couldn't figure a way forward without betraying her.

CHAPTER FIFTEEN

TWO DAYS AFTER the fire, Alannah paced before the hearth at the heart of the feasting hall as Emer swept the stone floor, the swish of her broom at odds with Alannah's footfalls.

"Why has no one come?" she asked aloud. "Why hasn't the king sent someone to investigate the fire?"

It made no sense. The king had gone to such effort to have it built over the past months—why would he not come to defend it?

Ath Luain was a modestly sized town, if indeed the term 'town' could reasonably be applied. It was more a smattering of farms surrounding a marketplace near the river. Even with its growth over her lifetime, Alannah knew it was almost an afterthought of a settlement.

Aside from the ford, which made it a frequent thoroughfare for travelers and a logical stopping place for merchants, there wasn't much reason to visit. It saw its fair share of trade, but couldn't hold a candle to the hubs like Dyflin and Luimneach. The farming was fair, but, again, nothing compared with the lush fields in Midhe to the east.

All of this, combined with the town's proximity to the kingdom's capital at Cruachan Aí, meant that it fell directly into the jurisdiction of the king himself. He visited Ath Luain frequently, hosting other kings and generally using it as a meeting place. There was no petty king ruling here—only Cahill. So why did he not come?

"You'll wear a track in the floor," Emer called, hanging up the broom. She joined Alannah by the hearth, but instead of pacing she sat on one of the wooden stools and stoked the crackling flames.

"He needs to *do* something." Alannah sat on a stool beside her sister.

"I'm certain he has a perfectly good reason for delaying." Emer prodded a glowing coal back to life. "Perhaps there was an attack we don't know of, or he was called away and hasn't heard yet."

Alannah perked up, her sister's words rolling around in her mind. "Has anyone sent a runner to him?"

Emer laughed. "How should I know? I'm not in charge."

Her thoughts ignited like the flames Emer stoked, flickering from one to the next. She shot to her feet once more. "It didn't burn very long," she thought aloud. "We put it out almost as soon as the smoke rose high enough to be seen at Cruachan Aí. Perhaps no one saw it at all."

Though Alannah would wager her year's earnings that Oran was behind the fire, the king still needed to know about it. And it would be far easier to get that bastard his comeuppance if the king, too, learned of his treachery.

"That's very possible," Emer agreed. "And if no one from Ath Luain went there to tell the king, then he'd have no way of knowing."

"Precisely!" She turned to regard her sister, rising to move onto her next task. They were alike in that one way—neither could sit still when there was work to be done. Their mother and aunts had been the same, and it was a trait that served them well in managing their hostelry. "Which is why I'm going to do it."

Emer's chestnut eyes swung to her. "That's a long trip to take on your own."

"It's only two days' walk. We've gone there before."

"Aye." Emer's hands went to her hips, and Alannah knew she was in for it. "We've gone there with a group of twenty or more for the fair, or with family to trade. No matter how much you train with those bards, you'd still be a woman walking there on her own. There's brigands and boars and wolves and—"

"I get it," Alannah interrupted her. "No need to continue."

"You can do anything, Alannah." Emer walked over, taking her hands. "But you shouldn't do this alone."

"Speaking of 'alone,' I don't know how I feel about you being here all by yourself for four days or more." Alannah had been so concerned over the attack on the bridge, she hadn't considered how her absence might impact her sister. "Oran will realize I'm not here, and—"

"And that's why we'll ask those nice gentlemen to keep an eye on things while you're gone. They're very sweet," Emer smiled. "I'm sure they'll help. In fact, Conan might be a good one to ask to travel with you."

The thought of a several day journey alongside Conan set Alannah's pulse racing. "You're trying awfully hard to push me into him, you know that?"

Emer laughed, walking to the kitchen and pulling several onions out of storage. "Someone has to look out for you. Lord knows you won't do it yourself."

Alannah rolled her eyes, watching her sister set to chopping for the evening meal. "I'll go speak with them, and I'll plan to leave in the morn."

"I'll pack you something tasty." Emer's round face lit like a lantern.

Alannah headed out the front doors, stopping to plant a quick kiss on her kindhearted sister's cheek. She didn't know what she'd do without Emer. She knew that after their training in the morning, the men bathed and then were gone until dinner time. Sometimes they stayed in their cottage. Other times she hadn't a clue where they were, and it honestly wasn't any of her business.

She stopped by their cottage first, but there was no sign of the men so she headed down the path towards Ath Luain. She hadn't walked for two minutes before she heard them chattering down the way.

Conan noticed her first, his slate grey eyes pinning her in place. A smoldering half-smile curved one side of his very tasty lips. She couldn't stop herself from imagining what it would feel like to have them on her skin again.

"I was hoping to speak with you," she called, ignoring the way her stomach fluttered when Conan hurried to walk beside her.

"I'm always hoping to speak with you," he grinned.

Behind them, one of the men snorted, clearly suppressing a laugh.

"I need to travel to Cruachan Aí, and Emer thought it would be safer if I didn't go alone."

Conan's dark brow creased. "Emer is correct," he agreed. "Why do you need to go?"

"I don't think anyone has told the king that the bridge was burned, and we need him to send men to look into it. If it wasn't an accident, we need to find and stop whoever's responsible."

A flicker of something crossed his face, gone as soon as it came. "Perhaps he's already looked into it and deemed it an accident."

Alannah shook her head. "I asked Glasny today, and he said he's not seen any of the king's men come by. He also didn't know of anyone going to tell him what happened, and Glasny knows most of the goings-on in Ath Luain."

"I'm afraid we can't go with you," Illadan answered from behind them. "We have business in Ath Luain to see to."

"I know," she ventured slowly, "that Conan has no desire to be seen by the king. He could stay outside the rath, if that would help."

Illadan's face softened, but his resolve did not. "He must stay here, Alannah. Regardless of his past with the king."

Conan frowned, biting his lower lip. "I'm sorry," he said softly. "I wish I could help."

Alannah felt as though someone had laid an iron cloak over her, smothering her kindled hopes. "You still can. While I'm gone, someone needs to make sure Oran stays away from Emer."

"And Eoghan," Conan added darkly. "Your sister seems to attract trouble."

"Honey attracts all manner of creatures, even the less desirable."

"True enough," Conan chuckled. "We will keep her safe in your absence, but who will protect you?"

Alannah patted the sword her brothers had made for her. "I've got all the protection I need right here. I was simply trying to assuage my sister's worries."

"The road can be dangerous, even for those who are paid for their skill in combat."

"I'll be fine." She flashed him her best smile, hoping to pacify his concerns as well. "I've been there many times. I know the way well."

Conan didn't argue, but the muscles worked along his sharp jaw. And it wasn't as though Alannah was happy about it, either. Of course she'd prefer the pleasure of his company to four days of travelling alone. But Illadan was clearly in charge, and he'd just as clearly opposed the idea.

At least Emer wouldn't be left unprotected. With her sister guarded by this band of giants, Alannah could at least travel with some peace of mind.

CHAPTER SIXTEEN

THERE WAS NO way in hell he was actually letting her go to Cruachan Aí alone. There was also no way that Illadan was going to let Conan accompany her, so as they entered their cottage at The Hart's Rest, Conan prepared for a battle.

Illadan beat him to the first punch.

"You cannot risk being seen in Cruachan Aí," he whispered. "Anyone from your father's household will recognize you, and even outside the city you would be at risk of discovery. Aside from all of that, you need to spend less time with her. Already she knows too much, too many details."

"She cannot go alone," Conan growled. "You understand as I do the dangers of travel for anyone, let alone a beautiful woman by herself."

Illadan didn't flinch. "Then help her find an alternative."

"What of you?" Conan turned to Finn, Dallan, and Ardál. "What if it was one of you and not me?"

"They're as familiar with Cahill's court as you are," Illadan argued. "Or have you forgotten that we just spent all winter drinking and playing at knucklebones with them in Dyflin? Every one of the Fianna is on a first-name-basis with half Cahill's household guard."

Damn. He was right, as usual. Conan strode the length of the small cottage, running a hand over his face and trying not to explode in frustration. Someone had to go with her. She must not have many options or she'd not have come to them, for they'd only been in town a few days. But Illadan was correct—none of the Fianna should go anywhere near Cruachan Aí. If they were seen, it would jeopardize their mission.

Conan stopped his pacing, spinning to face Illadan. If they were *seen*, it would jeopardize their mission. "What if I followed in secret?"

"What would be the purpose of that, precisely?" Illadan challenged, crossing his arms. "Would you not be following her to protect her in the case of trouble?"

"Of course," Conan replied. "But she'd not know I was there."

Illadan leveled him a pointed look. "Unless there was trouble."

In which case Conan would have no choice but to make his presence known in order to help Alannah. Grumbling, Conan renewed his pacing once more. "Are you suggesting that I allow ill to befall her in order to remain hidden?"

"I'm suggesting that you find someone else entirely to accompany her, or convince her not to travel at all."

With no better ideas at hand, Conan left the little cottage in search of Alannah. He didn't like the idea of sending someone else with her, but perhaps she knew of someone capable of protecting her. He'd feel a good deal better doing it himself, but Illadan was right. If something *did* go wrong, he'd have no choice but to reveal himself and endanger their mission.

He found her in the hall, wiping down the tables before the evening meal. It was the calm before the storm, the quiet before the crows descended for the feast. Emer quietly tended a stew pot over the hearth, smiling at him before returning her attention to the pot. The rich scent of lamb mingled with the tang of fresh herbs and the aroma of freshly-baked bread. Conan's mouth watered at the promise of the meal to come.

Alannah didn't halt her work, though he knew she'd seen him enter the hall. Her dark braid fell over her shoulder as she scrubbed a table near the kitchen, her focus entirely on her task.

"Is there anyone else who might be able to accompany you to Cruachan Aí?" he asked, grabbing a towel from the small table in the kitchen and helping her clean.

"I could always ask Glasny," she answered, keeping her voice low. "But he doesn't have anyone else to mind the alehouse in his absence. I'm not sure he'd agree."

"Is he capable with a sword?" Conan matched her tone.

Alannah paused long enough to shrug, her shoulders drawing his eyes to her chest. Even in the loose-fitted léine she wore, Conan easily spied the familiar swell of her breasts—something he'd thought of often since the night they'd arrived in Ath Luain. He may have gotten to spend the night with them, but he'd not even seen them in the blinding darkness of the room.

"I've never seen him fight, but he's big enough. He was a friend of my father's."

Conan frowned. If he was old enough to be her father and she'd never seen the man fight, he doubted this Glasny would be an acceptable replacement for his company.

"You're strangely quiet," she observed, pinning him with a cornflower blue stare. "Conan the bard always has something to say."

He couldn't suppress a grin at her prodding. "I don't like the idea of you traveling without someone who can protect you, and this Glasny fellow doesn't sound promising in that regard."

"Haven't you been training me every day to protect myself?" She stopped wiping now, placing both hands down on the table and glaring at him.

In spite of her strong stance and the implication of her question, Conan noted a tone of vulnerability in her manner and voice.

"I've trained for years, and I don't travel alone." While true, it wasn't for the same reasons.

"You would, though," Alannah muttered, calling him out. "Do you truly believe me incapable of defending myself? I have a sword. I have at least as much training as my brothers had before they left for battle. I think you doubt me because I'm a woman."

"I don't doubt you," Conan tried. "I simply worry over you, as I'm certain you worry over your brothers."

She bit her bottom lip, clearly plotting another argument, so Conan pressed on. Maybe he could convince her not to go at all.

"Let me ask you this. If I were going into battle, even though you know that I'm skilled in combat, would you not still worry over me?"

She cocked her head irritably, looking at him from under her lashes. "Of course."

"I wouldn't see that as you doubting my skill, but rather as a sign of your great affection for me."

"And would my great affection for you stop you from going into battle?" she challenged.

"It would not," he answered carefully, "were the battle a necessity. But your journey is not one of necessity."

"You don't believe it's important to notify the king of an attack on his kingdom? To request aid in the face of a potential threat?" she hissed, still keeping her voice down. "What if the next attack is on the town itself? How could you know whether it's necessary or not until it's too late?"

How, indeed. Conan worked beside her, silently brooding. He couldn't argue with her on that point. For, though he did know for a fact that the people responsible for the fire on the causeway would not be attacking the town proper, he couldn't very well tell her as much.

"I'll be just fine, Conan," she assured him as they finished up the last table. "Just make sure my sister is safe until I return."

Conan watched her take up her usual post near the back entry to the hall, ready to guard Emer for the next few hours. The rest of that evening and long into the night, Conan wrestled with his conscience, unwilling to accept that Alannah would be traveling on her own. There wasn't a high risk of her getting into trouble, but the risk existed nonetheless.

As dawn blushed along the eastern horizon, Conan reached a

decision. He wouldn't be able to live with himself if something happened to her while she traveled. Aye, they weren't courting, and they'd hardly been involved since that first night other than training together in the mornings. But Conan's thoughts drifted to her more than they didn't since that night they spent together. He didn't have to be courting a woman to be concerned over her safety, and there was no denying that his worries only grew the more he contemplated her journey.

The odds of trouble finding Alannah were small and, therefore, so was the possibility of her discovering that he'd followed her. Not only that, but when Illadan undoubtedly laid into him over his disobedience, Conan would remind him of their oath to protect those in need. Alannah had even asked for his help, and according to his oath, he couldn't deny her. Which was good, because shortly after she took her leave that morn, Conan snuck out of Ath Luain after her.

CHAPTER SEVENTEEN

T HE TWO-DAY JOURNEY northwest to Cruachan Aí went well enough. It rained in the morning both days, but by afternoon the sun peeked through the slate-colored clouds and Alannah's clothes dried enough that she didn't freeze while she slept. Nothing bothered her, human or otherwise.

She'd been to Cruachan Aí many times. The king held a fair there every year with games and dancing and more merchants than she'd ever cared to count. Folk came from all nine kingdoms to the great fair at Cruachan Aí. Alannah wondered absently if Conan had ever been there. Perhaps she'd even heard him perform. It wouldn't surprise her—the fair was a widely attended event—but sadness crept into the edges of her mind when she thought of having been there with him and not known it.

Though she'd visited every year for much of her life, Alannah had never before had cause to go directly to the king's rath. It was enormous, putting her small hostelry to shame. Easily twice the size of The Hart's Rest, the king's hall was built in the same ancient style as the inn, though it was itself an ancient structure. A massive dome woven of hazel branches and covered in thatch spread over the entire rath, the circular enclosure denoting the king's immediate residence. Outside the rath's tall palisades, a town that dwarfed Ath Luain sprawled across green hillsides, reaching in meandering paths toward the fields of oat and flax and barley that encircled it.

A pair of guards holding steady spears before their stern faces stood watch at the entrance to the rath. Much like The Hart's Rest, a long path led to double doors along the hall's outer wall.

Alannah expected the guards to stop her from entering, slowing so that she could answer any questions they might have of her. When they didn't appear concerned, she opened the heavy bronze door and stepped into the royal hall at Cruachan Aí.

She stood just inside the doorway for several moments, allowing her eyes to adjust to the dimmer light inside the magnificent hall. Where The Hart's Rest had one outer compartment behind a wattle half-wall, the king's hall had no less than five compartments that circled the main room, the bronze walls rippling outward like waves around a tossed stone. Each of the compartments was wide enough to accommodate braziers, so that they weren't too dark even though the bronze walls barred the hearth light, in addition to ample space for walking.

Another pair of guards stood in her path, near the walls of the third compartment. They, also, didn't move, but from behind them a man appeared. Thin and frail-looking, he had smoky hair tied in a knot and a long beard that matched. He wore a léine of forest green.

"Welcome to Ráth Cruachan," he greeted her. His voice sounded like two stones rubbed together. "I am Eamon, steward of this royal hall. What brings you here today?"

They must get many visitors, as he didn't seem surprised at all by her appearance in the hall. Alannah straightened her shoulders, drawing herself upward. "I bring a message to the king from Ath Luain."

Eamon nodded solemnly. "The king is away, but I can see if the prince will receive you. Is that acceptable?"

"It is, thank you." Alannah felt the urge to fidget at the formality, but managed to keep her hands at her sides.

Eamon disappeared back into the main hall, behind the guards and out of her sight. The murmur of voices trailed toward her, but Alannah couldn't make out any of the words. She stood awkwardly, staring straight ahead and wondering if it would be more or less uncomfortable to make eye contact with the guards or let her gaze wander to take in the splendor surrounding her. Happily, Eamon's return spared her from the decision.

"My Lordship Teague, eldest son of King Cahill, will see you now. What is your name?"

She told him, then followed the steward past the rest of the bronze walls and their accompanying compartments, glancing down each as they passed and wondering what she'd find if she wandered that direction. After the final compartment, they entered the main hall, where a hearth as wide as Conan was tall drenched the cavernous room with warmth and light. Instead of stools, elegant wooden chairs surrounded the beckoning flames, draped with blankets and furs. The rest of the room held tables and several other circles of chairs.

At one of the tables to Alannah's left, a group of men played games and drank. On the far side of the room, nearer to the hearth, several women in elegant dresses worked on mending. One woman skillfully embroidered a rainbow of colorful threads into a dress. In two of the chairs next to the hearth, facing the doorway where Alannah entered, were a pair of men who looked near her own age—likely close to thirty or just past. It was to these men that Eamon led her.

"My lord, this is Alannah nic Lorcan of Ath Luain, here to bring you a message." He bowed, backing away and gesturing Alannah forward.

"What is your trade, Alannah?" A tall, fit man with long, dark hair that reminded her of Conan's tilted his head curiously at her.

"My sister and I own a guesting house in Ath Luain," she answered. "The Hart's Rest. King Cahill graciously permitted us to rent the land from him to build it four years ago."

"Does that manner of work require you to wear trews and carry a sword?"

"No, lord. I do it to more easily protect my sister. Men have a tendency to lose their good sense around her. The sword knocks it back into them."

He and the man beside him, smaller of stature and with curly pale hair, laughed at her reply. "And the trews?"

"They make the wielding of the sword and the escorting of the rowdy men easier. Long skirts tend to get in the way." He certainly was taking a great interest in her choice of attire. But, then, it was a little unusual to wear to call on the royal family. If she'd given it more thought, Alannah would have brought one of her nicer gowns to wear. She'd been in such a hurry to relay the message that she hadn't stopped to think about bringing presentable clothes.

"I'm certain they do," he smiled. "What is the message you bring to your king? I will relay it myself upon his return."

"The causeway at Ath Luain was attacked. Someone tried to burn it, but we put the fires out before much damage could be done."

His dark brow furrowed, oddly reminding her of Conan yet again. It seemed even miles away she couldn't keep the roguish bard from her thoughts.

"Have any subsequent attempts been made to destroy it?" the prince asked.

Alannah shook her head. "No, lord, though I fear they are forthcoming. I came here to ask for men to help us guard it against further attacks."

Teague brought a hand to his face, stroking the short, dark beard on his chin and staring into the fire.

Alannah waited, giving him time to decide what course of action he believed best.

"How badly did it burn?" he asked. "I imagine that even if it is still usable, it may need repairs."

Alannah fought the urge to shuffle her feet, forcing herself to keep looking toward the prince. "I didn't inspect it very closely, lord." She should have, though. How had she not thought to do so?

He nodded, his eyes still pensive. "I believe my father would wish to inspect it himself, but he won't be returning for some time. I will come to Ath Luain in his stead. You own a hostelry, you say? Have you any rooms free?"

"Aye, lord, but they're far too small for a prince. We have but one stone cottage, and it's already occupied. I'm building another, but it isn't ready yet."

"I will come see the available rooms and decide for myself what is fit for a prince," he declared. "You have a few days to prepare, as I have business to attend here first. I will bring men with me to stand guard until the culprits of the fire are found."

Alannah bowed, feeling much like a goose pretending to be a swan. "Thank you, lord. We'll look forward to your visit."

"Thank you, Alannah, for taking it upon yourself to relay the news of the fire. Until I arrive, you have my permission to set a watch and investigate it as you see fit. If you wish, you may sleep here before returning to Ath Luain. Eamon," he called.

The steward stepped forward beside Alannah.

"If she wishes to stay, she may have a room in the fifth compartment."

Alannah thanked him again, her curiosity getting the better of her nerves. She wasn't about to pass by the opportunity to see what lay beyond the bronze walls, no matter how out of place she felt in a hall of kings. If Emer was alone back in Ath Luain, Alannah would not have stayed. But knowing that the bards were keeping watch in Alannah's stead made her comfortable accepting the prince's offer of accommodation.

Eamon led her to a room she estimated to be about a quarter of the way around the outside wall of the hall, in the fifth and outermost compartment. The flickering lights of the braziers bounced wildly off the bronze walls, casting dancing shadows as they passed.

The sleeping cubicles were modest, smaller than the individual roundhouses at The Hart's Rest, but far more luxurious. Alannah estimated that the corridor through the compartment was about four feet wide, and the cubicle about six feet in both directions. It looked as though the fourth compartment was made up entirely of little cubicles, which were accessed by doors in the fifth. Eamon opened one such door, casting into view a small but tidy room with its own brazier. A pallet covered in linens lay in one corner of the room, a stool and cupboard in another.

"We dine at the none bell. I'll have a meal sent to you."

She thanked Eamon, content with the offer of food and a warm bed and the opportunity to see the inside of the royal hall. Teague hadn't invited her to dine with them, after all. The use of a room alone had been most generous. Her mission completed, Alannah laid down on the soft pallet, wondering how in the world she was going to get the hostelry ready to host a prince in only a few short days.

CHAPTER EIGHTEEN

THE FOLLOWING MORN, Alannah left early. With no window in her chamber, she hadn't the faintest notion of the hour when she awoke. All she knew was her stomach rumbled and she didn't want to overstay her host's gracious welcome. Emer had packed her enough food for a full sennight, in case she encountered any delays, so Alannah had plenty of oat cakes and smoked salmon to eat as she walked, and no need at all to bother the prince for food.

Indeed, she didn't bother the prince at all, even to thank him for his hospitality and fare him well, for Eamon informed her that he was in a meeting. Instead, she asked Eamon to relay her gratitude and started on the long road back to Ath Luain.

The weather proved far fairer for the return journey. Instead of a quiet but insistent pattering of raindrops, the warm sun accompanied her for the morning. It looked as though it would be a pleasant trip until just after her break for the midday meal.

Alannah walked through a thick forest, with ancient oaks and hawthorns whose branches leaned and twisted in a timeless dance. Scrubby spindle bushes and wild roses claimed much of the forest floor, mosses and ferns filling in the empty spots. A rustling caught her attention, her ears reaching in pursuit of the sound. When she heard nothing more, she kept walking, ignoring the shiver that coursed down her spine.

Another rustle, this one continuous and heading in her direction.

Alannah scanned the forest on either side of her, drawing her sword.

The noise continued.

The blood rushed from her head, her stomach clenching in anticipation. The sounds came from behind her. Alannah spun, sword at the ready, to find three men coming at her.

Not a one looked friendly. All of them were scarred. All carried weapons. All wore greedy sneers. They rushed her all at once.

A buzzing filled her ears. She parried the first blow. The sound of steel rang in her ears.

The second man shoved her to the ground, laughing, as the third dropped his sword and kicked hers far from reach.

Alannah's stomach churned, nausea overtaking all other sensations. She was alone. No one was here to save her this time.

She prepared herself for a fistfight. It wasn't going well, but she didn't have to be winning to keep fighting. Balling her fists, she readied herself to attack the first man to try to rob her—for there was no doubt in her mind that these men were bandits.

One leaned over her and she landed a punch to his face with a satisfying crack. Her hand throbbed, but she didn't stop, drawing back to strike him again.

A scream drew both of their attention. The man above her turned to look, as did Alannah.

Her mouth fell open. Relief washed over her even as her heart stuttered. Conan strode toward them, the bandit's two companions already lying on the road. The third bandit jumped away from her, running from Conan. Shifting his grip on the sword, Conan threw it like a spear, skewering the man through his back. Then, as though she'd simply stumbled and fallen, he offered her an arm up.

"How is it every time I find you, you're getting into a fight?" He tossed her an easy grin.

Her fingers tingled as she gripped his hand, rising to her feet. She didn't want to let him go. "I've only started one of them."

The grin slipped from his angular face. "Are you alright?" He spun her, still holding her hand, inspecting her.

"I'm fine," she assured him. Her hands moved to rest on his hard chest, everything in her screaming to be nearer to him, until a stray thought took hold. He'd told her he couldn't come on the journey, yet here he stood—two days' walk outside of Ath Luain. "How are you here?"

CONAN STILL HELD tight to her slim waist, his hands savoring the feel of her hips beneath them. He forced himself to breathe deeply. She was safe. She was alright. He'd waited as long as he could bear before interfering in the fight, for Alannah preferred the chance to defend herself. But when the men had disarmed her and descended around her, Conan could wait no longer.

Taking one final breath he answered her question. "I may have snuck away, and just in time, it would seem."

He'd had the better part of two days to come up with an explanation. Alannah was both quick and clever, and he knew she'd ask. As he couldn't tell her the entire truth, he decided to include as much of it as he was able. She couldn't know that he'd left right after her and tracked her without going into Cruachan Aí, but everything else was fair game.

Her blue eyes, the same color as the clear spring sky above, widened. "You didn't get Illadan's permission?"

"He wouldn't give it." He raised a hand to brush her flushed cheek, unable to stop touching her. "I fear I may be in a bit of trouble when we return."

Her lips pursed temptingly. "I will speak on your behalf. There will be no trouble."

Conan lost himself in eyes like a sunlit sea, the brightest azure. If only he wasn't leaving in a few short weeks, he might do more than bed this woman.

If only he weren't trying to burn down the causeway that helped her business thrive, he might say he cared for her.

"What are you thinking?" Her hands gripped his léine, pulling him so close that he could feel her against him.

"I was thinking that you make me want things I cannot have."

It was strange to feel such hesitation to kiss a woman he'd already bedded. But when they'd shared that first night, it had been purely for the joy of it. Now, as he debated how she might react to a simple kiss, Conan understood how deeply their relationship had changed since then.

Bedding her had been fun.

But kissing her would change everything.

Her gaze fell to his lips, and Conan seized the opening. He moved slow this time, giving her plenty of opportunity to stop him.

She didn't.

His lips brushed hers tenderly, a whispered caress. He felt a connection forming between them, as though they were tied to opposite ends of the same rope, pulled ever closer.

Her fingers wove through his hair, her mouth parting as she kissed him right back.

Heat flooded Conan's body, a familiar hunger rising from deep within. He should stop. He knew he should cease this madness. Instead, he ran his hand down her shoulder, sliding over her breast to land on her waist. He dreamed of this body every night. He craved it every day.

Just as he was contemplating sneaking off into the trees with her, Alannah pulled back. "I can't," she whispered. "Just one night, remember?"

Conan released a shaky exhale. She was right. He was in the middle of sabotaging her only source of income. And even if he wasn't, his loyalties lay with Brian and the Fianna, his home in Cenn Cora. He'd be leaving far too soon to let this continue. "Just one night."

And one kiss.

CHAPTER NINETEEN

TWO DAYS LATER, Conan and Alannah walked up the worn path to The Hart's Rest. Alannah couldn't decide if she were grateful or disappointed that Conan hadn't tried any sort of intimacy after that kiss. On the one hand, she felt as though a current pushed her ever towards him, demanding that she give into her growing feelings for him. On the other, however, Alannah knew full well that there could be nothing between them except however many nights they shared together before he left. And, more and more, it was the leaving that was the problem. For the longer he stayed and the more moments they passed together, the more Alannah realized that this man could break her heart if she let him.

They arrived during the evening meal. Alannah threw open the doors, which felt smaller after having visited the splendid Rath Cruachan, to find all the comforts of home. Emer ferried platters laden with food among the six tables, stuffed to bursting with diners. Finn and Ardál played a soft tune. Illadan and Dallan stood by either door, keeping watch as Alannah had requested. Illadan was the closest and Alannah walked straight to him, determined to defend Conan.

When they approached, Illadan glared at Conan, his dark countenance promising a serious discussion. "You have some explaining to do."

"He does not," Alannah positioned herself between the two giants. "I would have been killed had he not disobeyed you, so I will thank you for use of your man and ask that he not be punished for saving my life."

"I caught up to her when she'd just left Cruachan Aí," Conan explained. "I found her just in time to accompany her on the journey back."

Illadan's features relaxed. "I see," he drawled, still glaring at Conan. "Perhaps your punishment can be mitigated, then."

"What will you have him do?" Alannah had hoped to erase any censure entirely, but lessening it would have to suffice.

"He'll be saving you the trouble of minding the horse stalls until we leave," Illadan declared. "But should he choose to continue disobeying direct orders, I'm afraid I'll have no choice but to punish him accordingly."

"He won't," Alannah hurried, answering on Conan's behalf. It was her own fault he'd come so close to such a punishment, and she'd not be the reason he fell out of favor with Illadan.

She still found it odd how military they seemed to be for a group of bards, but she supposed if they'd all trained for years and served together, it was easier to maintain old habits than grow too lax.

Illadan nodded, still frowning. "How did your journey go? Did you speak with the king?"

"He wasn't in Cruachan Aí, but I spoke with his son, Teague. He was very kind and understanding, and he promised to bring men here and investigate the fire."

"He's coming here himself?"

Alannah couldn't suppress a smile. "Aye, he said he wanted to survey the damage and order repairs. He even let me stay in the rath overnight."

Illadan didn't look nearly as happy as she'd expected for such good news. "Excellent," he muttered.

CONAN WATCHED ALANNAH hurry to Emer, embracing her sister in an enthusiastic hug. Once she was out of earshot, he turned to Illadan.

"I'm sorry I disobeyed orders."

Illadan sighed, the typical, put-upon sound that accompanied most of his interactions with the Fianna. "You're a good man, a good warrior, a loyal friend." He pitched his voice low, ensuring they wouldn't be overheard. "I'm concerned that you're becoming too involved personally with this mission to remain professional."

Conan swallowed hard. Had he not been thinking something similar over the past two days? The closer he grew to Alannah, the guiltier he felt over all the things he hid from her.

His identity.

His true reason for visiting Ath Luain.

That he'd been the one to attack the bridge, and that he intended to do so again.

That he was doing all of these things, knowing full well how important the bridge was to her.

"Your silence does naught to ease my concerns," Illadan continued. "What else do you know of their plans?"

A pang of guilt struck Conan's chest once more, but he answered as Illadan commanded. "She's going to put together a watch for the causeway. Teague will contribute men, and will repair any damages. He intends to come to the hostelry in a day or two."

Illadan's brow furrowed deeper. "That's going to be a problem. We'll need to discuss that tonight." He laid a heavy hand on Conan's shoulder. "Get us on the watch. We'll take as many nights as needed."

Conan nodded, looking down at his feet. His loyalty was to Brian and the Fianna, yet he couldn't help but feel that he betrayed Alannah—which was ridiculous, because they weren't even lovers. And for good reason, clearly.

"Are you ready?" Alannah asked, joining him and Illadan by

the front doors of the hostelry. "I want to get to Glasny's before it gets too wild."

"What's at Glasny's?" Illadan asked.

"We're recruiting men to watch the bridge until Teague's reinforcements arrive," Conan explained.

Illadan turned to Alannah. "We will take as many nights on the watch as you need."

"Thank you." She beamed at them both.

Glasny's alehouse was on the far side of the causeway, along the eastern bank of the Sionnain. A large rectangular stone building with a thatched roof, Conan wouldn't have known it was anything other than a house if Alannah hadn't led them there. Slats of wood covered with thatch pitched toward the road from the roof, creating a sheltered outdoor space with tables and extra seating. Conan wondered how often it saw use in a town as small as Ath Luain. Would the entire town need to turn out to fill the tables?

Inside, warm light from a central hearth illuminated an open room with tables in every shape and size, chairs and benches as mismatched as the rest of it. About a dozen men and women milled about, carrying drinks, playing at knucklebones, or sitting at tables laughing. Behind a counter to the right of the door, a middle-aged man with a burly build and peppered beard filled empty cups. When the man caught sight of Alannah, his face came to life.

"Finally taking me up on that drink?" he shouted, waving them over and filling two cups with ale. He passed one to each of them as they took up positions by the counter.

"Still here on business, Glasny," Alannah laughed, sliding her cup back across the smooth wooden surface. "We're setting a watch at the causeway until the prince can get here."

Conan took a long drink of the ale, mild and sweet with less warmth than he expected. It wasn't bad, though he wondered if it were cut with water to inhibit patrons from getting too deep into their cups.

"Who's he?" Glasny glowered at Conan, ignoring Alannah's request for watchmen. "I've not seen you before."

"He's alright," she assured him. "He's one of the bards staying with us. They've been playing every few nights."

Glasny perked up at that, arms crossing across his barrel of a chest. "You've been hiding away bards? How is it they've not yet played at my alehouse?"

"Help us man the causeway, and we'll play any night you'd like," Conan offered, taking another drink of ale.

Glasny's beard lifted into a hairy smile. "Aye. You've got yourself a bargain." He took a step away from them, facing the room at large and shouting. "The next four men to volunteer as guards at the bridge get free drinks tonight!"

The room behind them sprang to life as men hustled to claim their spots.

Alannah beamed. "Thank you, Glasny."

"Happy to help." He turned to Conan. "I believe you owe me a performance."

"That I do," Conan agreed. "That I do."

CHAPTER TWENTY

THE FOLLOWING EVENING, Glasny's crowded tavern boasted the best entertainment in Ath Luain. The tables were pushed to the edges of the large room, drinks scattered to the point of confusion. But no one sat.

Every single person stood packed together, filling the tavern and dancing like souls possessed. There wasn't room to spin or turn or to do any sort of organized dancing, so Alannah and Emer satisfied themselves jumping and laughing and making the best of the music.

Alannah couldn't take her eyes off Conan. He played a bodhrán this time, his hands moving so fast they blurred as they kept the heady rhythm.

"Why aren't you still *having fun* with him?" Emer shouted at her. Even projecting her voice, Alannah could barely hear her.

"It was just one night of fun." Every time she said it, the words felt more hollow. Perhaps it was more of an excuse than an explanation.

"Well it shouldn't be," her sister replied.

Alannah slowed her dancing to catch Emer's eyes. "It has to be. I can't afford any distractions."

Emer's dark brows knitted. She grabbed Alannah's wrist and dragged her out of the crowd and to one of the abandoned tables. "Sit."

Alannah obeyed, shocked at Emer's uncharacteristic tone.

Emer sat beside her, placing a hand on Alannah's arm. "I'm

not going to disappear," she said gently. "I'm not going to die like Mom and Dad, or leave like Ossian and Osgar. You're not going to lose me—not for a long, long time."

"You can't know that," Alannah's voice caught. "And what of the inn? I can't just fool around all day while you work to keep us surviving."

Emer sighed. "I don't want you to survive. I want you to *live*. And if that means you let go of some responsibility while a handsome bard is in town, then so be it."

Alannah felt her arguments falling out from under her, but she wasn't ready to abandon her sister just yet. "But—"

"I *love* running the inn," Emer interrupted, holding up a finger. "I love cooking meals and taking care of people. I love making them smile and hearing their stories. And you can't shadow me everywhere like a hired guard. That's no kind of life for you."

"What if something happens to you?" At the same time that Alannah felt possibilities appearing on the horizon, panic filled her at the thought of Oran finally getting to Emer.

Her sister squeezed Alannah's hands. "Some things are beyond our control."

"That's not making me feel any better," Alannah groaned.

Emer smiled. "I have more than enough protectors with our current guests, even if one of them is otherwise occupied."

"You're incorrigible, do you know that? Why are you pushing so hard?"

Emer didn't hesitate. "Because I've never seen you as happy as you were the day he walked through our door. And I've never seen you look at anyone the way you look at him."

"You two look entirely too serious." Conan appeared beside them, frowning.

They both stood in a sad attempt to be closer to eye level with the giant.

"My sister was just lamenting her lack of a dance partner," Emer lied.

Alannah had never considered Emer underhanded or devious, but now she wondered just how well she knew her baby sister.

"Is that so?" Conan's lips lifted into a knee-melting smirk.

"It is *not*," Alannah corrected, gaping at Emer.

He offered her a callused hand. "Let's see if we can dance longer than Finn can play."

She still didn't know if she could trust him. She still didn't know if she should leave her sister. But, heaven above, did she want to dance with him.

She took a deep breath.

Then she took his hand.

HE COULDN'T ENDURE this torment any longer. One more night couldn't hurt, right? It wasn't as though he were any less distracted *not* bedding her. He could have a little more fun without risking their mission. It wasn't as though he intended to marry the woman, and he'd wager she felt the same.

As long as he kept his identity from her, what harm could come of it?

Finn should have been a master bard. Everything about his performance was masterful, and he'd never even apprenticed. Equally impressive was Ardál's ability to keep pace with him. Together, their music brought the entire building to life.

But Conan's attention turned only briefly to the music. Alannah became his entire world the moment she took his hand. He'd have to thank Emer later.

He pulled her right up against him to dance. In the crush of people surrounding them, they were hardly closer than anyone else. And it made it easier to put his hand in the small of her back. It was enough for now, though his fingers itched to explore her body all over again. He didn't dare anything more intimate—not until he knew how she was feeling.

Most of her dark tresses had fallen free of the braid she always wore, falling around her shoulders and dancing as much as she did. Today her shirt was blue and entirely too loose. Conan knew the exquisite body hidden beneath its generous folds and couldn't see any of it.

She leaned into him as they moved, her hand sliding on his chest.

They moved together in a way that put him in mind of a very different activity, her hips brushing his cock to the point of distraction as she swayed in front of him.

Bending his head, he whispered into her ear. "What if it was two nights?" He couldn't play this game any longer.

"Then you'd have to make it worth my while." She smiled against his cheek.

Desire flooded him, taking control of his mind and his body. As it turned out, Finn could, in fact, play longer than Conan could dance. Or longer than he was willing to dance, anyway, without sneaking Alannah away from the crowd.

He led her through the packed alehouse with every intention of taking her back to The Hart's Rest and tossing her onto the first bed he found. They were almost to the door when he felt the cool rush of wind sweep inside. His steps faltered when he saw the newcomer.

Teague.

He turned around slowly, not wanting to draw attention to himself. His brother hadn't seen him yet, for there'd been no eye contact nor sign of recognition. But it was only a matter of time. He needed to warn the rest of the men. Sighing in disappointment, Conan turned to Alannah.

"I need to tell the men we're leaving," Conan told her, pulling her quickly with him back toward the rest of the Fianna.

She didn't resist, following him with a nod of understanding.

Conan found Finn first, his blonde head sticking above the fray. He was too easy to spot. When they reached the men, Conan yanked Finn downward, hoping to afford him more cover.

"He's here. We need to leave." He whispered directly into Finn's ear, never letting Alannah's hand go.

Finn's sea-blue eyes scanned the room, widening for just a moment as he no doubt spotted Teague entering the crowded alehouse. "I'll let the men know."

Conan patted his shoulder and kept moving. Never turning back toward the front door, he led Alannah out the back.

"Why didn't we just use the front door?" she laughed. At least she wasn't overly suspicious of his quick turnaround.

Conan rejoined with an uneasy chuckle. He wasn't as good as Diarmid or Dallan at concealing his thoughts—or Cormac, Illadan, or Broccan, for that matter. Finn and Ardál were the only other Fianna who appeared to struggle keeping secrets.

"I just wanted to get out of there," he answered truthfully. At least he'd begun with the truth. "It was too crowded to keep going back and forth."

"Then let's get you somewhere more private," she purred, pulling him closer.

Conan's lips captured hers, rewarding her bold suggestion. "Now that sounds like an excellent idea."

CHAPTER TWENTY-ONE

S HE TOOK HIS hand, leading him to her own cottage and praying Emer stayed out a bit longer.

He closed the door. "What is it you want?"

Alannah grinned at him, settling onto the only proper bed they had at The Hart's Rest. Frames, mattresses, and pillows were too expensive to have in every room. "I want to see those muscles of yours," she told him. "I was robbed last time."

"As my lady wishes." He wiggled his brows playfully, taking his shirt off and tossing it unceremoniously onto the floor.

Her breath caught. All the training he did each day showed in every sculpted plane of his body. Alannah's fingers itched to touch them all.

He stalked toward her, his eyes clouded and his lips parted. His glorious body covered hers, his lips claiming her as his.

The last time they'd lain together, Alannah's body had wanted him. But now it was something much deeper, a part of her soul, that craved him. As he pulled her tunic over her head, Alannah realized that she didn't just want one night anymore.

She wanted every night.

Finally, her hands roamed his smooth chest, wandering across the ridges of his stomach and savoring every incredible inch. She'd tried so hard to stay away from him, to put enough distance between them that her heart wouldn't be at risk. Yet somehow she'd still ended up right back in his bed. By the time she reached the hem of his trews, she burned hotter than a blacksmith's forge.

"Not so fast." His callused palms cupped both her breasts. "I, too, was robbed."

Alannah's back arched of its own accord as first Conan's hands, then his mouth played with her sensitive nipples. The wet, warm heat of his lips, his tongue only fanned the growing flames. A breathy exhale escaped her as she dragged her hands across his shoulders.

All thought fled her. Only a coiling desire, an unquenchable need to fill the emptiness opening in her core remained. The very air around her pricked her sensitive skin.

Conan moved lower, his lips tasting her stomach, her hips, her thighs. When he reached the heat of her, he sucked and licked until she ached for him. His fingers joined his mouth, teasing her until she thought she might explode with need.

"Conan," she pleaded, just as she had that first night. She felt him smile against her.

"Always in a hurry," he chided, finally relenting his sweet torment and moving back on top of her. His lips found her neck as he entered her.

He moved slowly, languidly. The pressure of him inside her pleasured her at the same time as it teased of something more. He filled her so completely, so perfectly, that Alannah had no doubt that she belonged with Conan. He was her other half, in body and in spirit. How was she ever going to let him go?

But she was in no mood to be teased any longer. Wrapping her legs around his waist, she pulled him deeper inside her.

That proved his undoing. He moved faster, driving into her over and over. The intoxicating scent of leather and spice and *him*, stole what remained of her senses. It was just Conan and her and the feel of them together as the pressure inside her continued to build.

As before, his fingers found their way back to her core, swirling and rubbing until everything went dark, stars filling her vision and warmth pooling where his fingers worked their magic.

His cock tightened inside her as he thrust harder and deeper.

He lowered himself onto her, their bodies pressed together, as he found his own release.

Alannah knew that this changed everything about their relationship, but that idea no longer scared her. That he might be leaving someday soon, however, had her heart racing in panic. Wrapping her arms around him, Alannah closed her eyes, determined to soak up every minute of her time with Conan.

"Hello?"

Somewhere within the depths of her haze, Alannah registered the call from the main room.

"Is anyone still awake?"

"Damn," Alannah muttered under her breath, shifting so that she could move out from under Conan. She'd nearly fallen asleep. "I don't think Emer's back yet."

Conan roused quicker than she expected, considering her own drowsy state. He moved to let her up, grabbing her clothes and handing them to her before gathering his own.

"Wait for me," he ordered, his eyes dancing as they watched her dress. "It concerns me that someone's getting in so late."

"You and me both," she grumbled. This was *not* the ending she'd had in mind for the night.

Conan's warmth covered her back, his arms wrapping around her belly as he kissed her neck. The movement was so tender, sending a shiver rippling through her. It was the sort of thing a lover would do.

Was that what they were now?

Alannah's reservations weren't entirely gone, but she had to admit she liked the sound of that. She liked the way it made her feel even more. Turning in his arms, she pulled his face to hers, giving him a quick kiss before hurrying across the courtyard and into the common room.

A man with a thick, bushy beard stood warming himself by the fire. Of average height and stocky build, he wore trews that had seen better days and a léine in desperate need of a wash.

He turned when they entered the room. "Oh, thank goodness. I'm sorry to bother you so late, but I heard you might still have vacant rooms?"

Alannah was about to get the man signed in and settled, but Conan stepped in front of her.

"What business has you out so late?"

"I thought I could make it home by nightfall, but I'm afraid I miscalculated. I just need to stay long enough to sleep before I make the last few miles," he explained. "My unit was disbanded."

Alannah had to stop herself from jumping and clapping as Emer did when she was excited. "Are more men coming?"

"Aye, I was in one of the southernmost camps. The rest should follow over the next few days."

She stood in stunned silence, thanking the stars above.

Her brothers were finally coming home.

CHAPTER TWENTY-TWO

ONAN'S HACKLES FELL the moment the man mentioned his discharge. He turned toward Alannah, unsurprised to find her lips parted and her eyes full of hope. Nodding at the man, he took a seat to let Alannah get the visitor settled. The man's story felt true enough, but he wasn't about to leave her alone in a room with a grizzled warrior in the middle of the night, sword or not.

"We have a room for you," she assured him.

He waved a tired hand. "I'll stay in one of the cubicles here. I just need a good night's sleep and then I'm heading home."

"That'll only be a penny." Alannah stepped toward him. "My brothers are supposed to be among the men coming home. I don't suppose you know Ossian or Osgar?"

The man thought a long moment, squinting and cocking his head. "I can't say I recall the names," he said at last. "But it was a large unit. It's possible I simply never met them."

Alannah nodded, moving to show the man which cubicle was his and to get his payment. The hope was gone from her face, her shoulders sagging like a deflated waterskin.

Conan hoped they came home. It killed him that there wasn't a damn thing he could do to make sure they did, but he would help her question every returning soldier if needs be. Even if her brothers never came, they'd find out why. With every fiber of his being, he prayed it wouldn't come to that.

Sounds of conversation interrupted his thoughts. He recognized Emer's voice quickly, her bright, dulcet tone now familiar.

He sprang to action when he placed her companion's deep voice.

"I'm going to turn in the for the night." He pulled Alannah into a quick embrace, leaving her with a disappointingly chaste goodnight kiss and hurrying through the back door. When he reached the little stone cottage, unsettling silence greeted him.

Finn and Dallan sat, reclining on two of the pallets. Ardál stood staring out the narrow window.

Illadan laid in wait by the door and skewered him with a hazel glare. "We have a very serious problem."

"It's not like I invited him here," Conan shot back. His arms tensed, the muscles squeezing as though he held his sword. "No one saw me when I followed her."

Illadan ignored him, pacing toward the back of the cottage. "Not only is he already committed to helping our hostesses protect the bridge," he grumbled, "which means that if we did enlist his help, his quick turnabout on the matter would be suspicious, but he also has the potential to destroy both our secrecy *and* the mission itself."

"I think we need to tell him," Dallan declared from his pallet. He sat with his legs tented, his arms resting atop his knees.

Conan shook his head. "And give him fuel against us to use with Cahill?"

"He's working with us now," Dallan added, as though that made a bit of difference to Conan.

"It makes more sense for him to be in on the plan," Finn agreed. "That way if Cahill suspects anything, Teague can more effectively cover our tracks. And we can enlist his help in keeping our identities hidden from the women."

"And if he simply outs us and tells Cahill everything that's happened?" Conan pressed.

"Either he will or he won't," Ardál added unhelpfully.

Conan leveled him a look. He hardly ever spoke, and *that* was what he chose to add to the debate?

Ardál returned the look, unflinching. "Either he will prove the validity of his oath to Brian or he will out himself as untrustworthy. It's as good a time as any to discover where his loyalty truly lies."

That was a fair point, Conan admitted grudgingly. Sooner or later, Teague would be tested with sensitive information. He supposed discovering his brother's intentions sooner would be better than later. He still didn't trust the bastard, though, and he wasn't entirely certain one secret kept would be enough to earn it.

"It appears I'm outnumbered," Conan grumbled.

"He'll be less likely to betray us if we tell him," Dallan said.

They all stared at him skeptically. They might have agreed it was a worthwhile risk, but that didn't make any sense.

"How do you figure that?" Finn asked.

"If we don't tell him what we're up to and Cahill becomes suspect, it would be easy for Teague to tell him we were here and implicate us without us even knowing it. If we specifically give him the directive to cover it up, he'll feel the pressure from us knowing whether he did or didn't do it."

Illadan's eyes narrowed, wandering off in thought. "If we ask for his help, he'll no longer have the excuse of ignorance. I agree."

Knowing when he'd lost a battle, Conan sighed. "Fine. We tell him. How?"

Somehow it irked him even more that they would be telling Teague—a man he wouldn't trust with his lunch, let alone his life—while they worked even harder to keep it from Alannah and Emer. The women were far more trustworthy, and even if they learned the men's true identities, it didn't necessarily connect them with the bridge.

"We need to get him alone," Dallan replied, looking directly at Conan. "What if I distract Emer and you Alannah?"

Conan swallowed hard against the rancid guilt rising from his churning gut. He didn't like this plan at all. "What if we tell the women as well?"

Silence took up residence once more, all eyes flying to him.

Illadan brought the first challenge. "You must be joking."

"I trust them more than I do my brother," Conan continued.

"It's too risky." Ardál finally stepped away from his window. "Even if we only reveal our identities, your woman is actively searching for those responsible for the attack. It's only a matter of time before she puts it together."

He wasn't wrong, of course. Alannah was as clever as a fox and as driven as a hound on the hunt. "She's hardly my woman," was all Conan could think to argue.

"You're the only one of us who's bedded her," Dallan grinned. "She's more yours than ours."

Conan shook his head. Though something in his chest swelled at the idea, Alannah didn't *belong* to anyone, and he had a feeling she'd take exception to that choice of words. She may not belong to him, but he began to wonder if perhaps he belonged to *her*.

"Ardál, find out where Teague is staying. Tomorrow morning, Conan and Dallan will get the women out of the way and we will bring him in on the mission," Illadan ordered.

Ardál left without another word, stepping back inside the cottage almost as soon as he'd left it.

Illadan frowned at him, opening his mouth to ask the same question that hovered in Conan's mind.

"I found him," Ardál announced, pitching his voice low, quiet. He pointed straight at the front door toward the east, where Alannah and Emer's quarters lay across the cobblestone courtyard. "He's staying in that cottage."

CHAPTER TWENTY-THREE

ALANNAH PACED IN front of the fire for the hundredth time. They still weren't back, and the talk around Ath Luain was that most of the soldiers had returned by now.

"Unless you've learned magic, I don't think any number of steps will bring them back." Emer handed her a warm infusion of honey-sweetened peppermint with an even warmer smile. "Maybe they were further away than most of the others."

"Maybe." Something felt wrong, though. Off, in a way she couldn't name. "Have you seen the men yet this morning?"

Emer shook her head, clearing the last of the dishes from the morning meal. "I thought maybe they decided to run before they ate."

Alannah stopped pacing, her shoulders sinking. If that was true, then wouldn't Conan have told her as much? Perhaps he'd forgotten. Or perhaps, as per tradition, Alannah had once again chosen to open herself up to the wrong man. She'd been suspicious of him since they arrived because no bard needed to be so skilled with the sword. As a group, they acted odd as well, clearly deferring to Illadan in a way that didn't feel at all like a troupe of performers. Doubt threaded through her, cloying and grasping as her mind searched for answers just out of reach.

She'd been wrong about many men, many times, but never so terribly as when she'd agreed to meet with Oran. The last thing they needed was a repeat of that disaster or another deranged man attempting to destroy their livelihood.

Unable to work through such concerns adequately, Alannah allowed one, tentative question to slip out. "Do you ever feel that Conan acts…oddly?"

Emer set down the last dishes on the table in the kitchen, turning her full attention on Alannah. "Do you like him?"

A rush of warmth bloomed in Alannah's chest in spite of her myriad concerns over him. "I do," she sighed. "That's the problem."

"Aye," Emer agreed too quickly. "It is. You don't trust yourself after Oran. You've not let yourself get close to a man since, and honestly I don't blame you."

"You didn't answer my question," Alannah challenged.

"I did, though. I think that it doesn't matter what Conan does, odd or otherwise, because you're in desperate search of a reason not to let your heart back into the open." Emer's features softened. "Where it can be broken."

Alannah tsked. "That's ridiculous. I never loved Oran. I saw him for what he was as soon as we spent any length of time together."

"I never said you loved him," Emer broke into a maddeningly satisfied grin. "But I think you just did."

Alannah groaned, falling onto the nearest bench. "You're no help at all."

If possible, she'd only made matters worse.

Emer walked over, grabbing her hands and giving them a squeeze. "Stop looking for problems. Conan is a kind man. He and his friends have done nothing but help us since they arrived. Let yourself have this."

Before Alannah could process her sister's words, let alone decide how she felt about them, the man in question stepped in the front door. Dallan followed right behind him, and neither man looked like he'd just gone for a run.

Conan's dark brows furrowed the moment he laid eyes on her. "What's wrong?"

Her heart hammered in her chest, her pulse rising with each

step he took toward her. So many things. The way he made her feel. The way she wanted so badly to trust him yet somehow could not. The way he was looking at her now.

Instead, she settled on the easiest answer. "They're not back."

"Your brothers?"

She nodded, rising from the bench.

His lips tugged together thoughtfully. "Let's go find out why."

"Really? Don't you need to train?"

"Not as much as you need to know where your brothers are."

Emer shot her a pointed look before turning to Conan. "Are you sure you have to leave? I like having you around."

Conan tossed her a soft smile. "Unfortunately, I can't stay. But I can help you while I'm here."

Yet another reason to keep her heart guarded—or what remained of it. Conan clearly wasn't feeling as strongly about her, even if he'd taken her to bed again. He couldn't be if he was still so determined to leave. Alannah grabbed her cloak and drained the last of her drink, savoring the sweet drops of honey that fell from the bottom of the mug. She wasn't about to waste this opportunity worrying over the implications of her conversation with Emer.

She rounded on Conan. "I have an idea."

Instead of heading into town, Alannah took Conan farther west.

Toward their farm.

Or, rather, the home that used to be their farm. It had been so hard to live there the first year after their parents passed. Everything reminded her of the life they'd had together. The only thing that kept her going was the knowledge that her sister and brothers were counting on her. She had to be strong for them, especially Emer.

Leaving had been almost as hard as staying. She hadn't gone back since.

Conan walked beside her on a path she knew with her eyes

closed. Fields of tiny green plants lined either side of the narrow road. In a few months, they would grow into a sea of barley.

"Out of curiosity," he began when the cottage came in sight at the path's end.

Alannah answered before he could finish. "The family that bought our home had a son who joined with our brothers."

"This is the farm you sold?" He slowed, taking a longer look at the fields around them.

"Aye." Alannah gritted her teeth against the ache that rose in her chest at the sight of the front door opening. It was impossible not to imagine her mother behind it, even after all these years. She felt Conan's eyes on her.

He didn't say a word. He took her hand instead, giving it a squeeze.

"Alannah, is that you?" Nuala called from the open door. She hurried to meet them before they reached the house, walking back toward it with them. "I saw someone walking down the path there, but I never expected to see you all the way out here. What brings you? Oh, I'm Nuala, by the way," she added, smiling at Conan.

"Nice to meet you, Nuala. I'm Conan." He grinned at her, charming as ever.

But his smile didn't hold the same promise of mischief as it did when it was for her. That realization eased her chest a bit, but the ache didn't go away completely.

"I was wondering if Darragh had returned with the rest of the men," Alannah asked.

Nuala's face lit up like a bonfire. "Darragh!" she yelled. "Come out here, would you?"

A tall, lanky man with shaggy brown hair hurried out the door. He'd filled out since he left with her brothers, but he still had the same freckled face and fun-loving smile.

"Alannah." He ran over and lifted her into a giant hug.

Over his shoulder, she saw Conan's jaw clench. He didn't try to hide his glare, either.

If she didn't know any better, she'd say he was jealous. But that was ridiculous. They weren't even lovers, really. She'd bedded him twice, aye, and she'd grown entirely too fond of him. But they hadn't discussed anything more than that yet. And he still planned to leave.

He had no business being jealous, but Alannah couldn't suppress the way it made her chest swell knowing that he was.

"How are you?" she asked after Darragh set her back down. "When did you get back?"

"Just two days ago," he answered. "And I'm just fine. Had a few cuts and a close call or two, but I fared better than many."

"I'm just so glad he made it back to me." Nuala looked at her son like he was her whole world, then she turned to Alannah. "Have your brothers come back yet?"

Alannah swallowed. "That's actually why I came by. They haven't. I was hoping maybe you knew why."

Darragh's face went blank, then he perked up. "They were transferred," he said. "Almost as soon as we arrived at the fort. I don't know where, but they both left right away."

Air returned to her lungs. Conan placed a hand on the small of her back.

"They might still be alive," she breathed.

"Oh, I'm sure they're just fine," Nuala soothed, rubbing her arm. "They're strong and clever. Good men. They'll be alright. Do you want to come in? I can fix some porridge."

Alannah waved away her kindness. "No, thank you. I should get back and tell Emer." And there was no way she was ever setting foot in that house again. "Thank you, both of you."

Conan's hand never left her back as they turned and walked away. "Are you alright?"

"Of course," she answered automatically.

He stopped walking. "Emer's not here." His tone was soft but firm. "You don't have to put on a show of strength or hide your wounds. Now, are you alright?"

Her shoulders dropped in response. "No," she whispered. "I

don't think I am."

"Come here." He pulled her into his arms, wrapping her in the earthy scent of leather and the warmth of his body.

She buried her face in the hard plane of his chest. "I just really thought they'd come home. I thought I'd get to see them again."

Beneath her forehead, his heart pounded out a steady rhythm. She felt tension forming in his arms. Looking up, she saw it in his face, too. "What's wrong?"

"If Emer or one of your brothers had done something horrible, would you give them another chance?"

"Like what?" she asked. His tone intrigued her, like even though he spoke of her family, it applied to him in some way.

He blew out a heavy breath. "Betrayal, among other things."

Alannah froze, choosing her words carefully. "I suppose it depends on the betrayal."

She breathed in, long and slow and deep, filling her lungs and trying not to panic over the turn in conversation. When he still didn't speak, she filled the yawning silence.

"Is there something you want to tell me?"

"My brother," he began, his throat working. "My brother is not a good man, but everyone seems inclined to give him another chance."

Understanding dawned, followed by rippling relief. He wasn't speaking of himself. He was talking about his brother. "Except you."

He nodded. "Except me."

Now that she understood the context, she knew her answer without question. Alannah would always believe in her brothers, in Emer. They'd all let each other down at one point or another, sometimes more seriously than others. But they always showed up again, always made amends. Because, at the end of the day, they were all each other had.

"Do you believe that people can change?"

He looked down his nose at her, as though her answer surprised him. "With proper motivation, perhaps. I would like to, anyway."

"Then you have your answer. Maybe you didn't like who he was, but maybe you can learn to love who he is."

"Love is a stretch," he smiled. "But maybe I can give him a chance. A small one," he qualified as they continued walking.

"You should. You deserve a brother, regardless of whether he deserves a second chance. Who knows? Maybe he'll surprise you."

"Everything he does surprises me," Conan grumbled.

"You never talk of your family." Alannah didn't want to throw away what might be the only opportunity to learn more about the man currently holding her heart.

"I'm very close with two of my brothers and my sister. It's just my eldest brother and my parents who cause problems."

That was more than he'd said when last she asked. A dozen questions popped up in her mind like a bouquet springing to life. The eldest brother must be the one he'd asked about earlier.

"Where are your two brothers and sister?"

"My sister lives in Mumhain most of the time. Though she travels some, I know she prefers to be at home. My two brothers travel with me often, but they couldn't this time, unfortunately." He smiled sadly. "You would like them."

Alannah sensed a shift in his mood. Something about his siblings brought an uncommon melancholy to the sharp angles of his face, a strain to the set of his jaw. Rubbing his arm and scooting closer, she did her best to cheer him. "If they're anything like you, I'm certain I would."

Some of the shadows cleared from his face, but the silence stretched between them once more.

CHAPTER TWENTY-FOUR

THE FOLLOWING DAY, Alannah ran and sparred with them, but Emer needed help with the inn all afternoon. Conan didn't know what he'd expected—it wasn't as though he had the afternoon free to spend with her—but his heart sank nonetheless.

He gathered more tinder with the Fianna, grabbed a quick meal, then he and Ardál headed to the bridge for their first watch. The sun hung low, but didn't quite touch the horizon.

The stars poked through the mass of clouds, a mat of thin wisps propelled by a wicked northerly wind.

"A storm's rolling in," Ardál announced, eyeing the western sky. "A big one."

"I'd wager no one will try burning the bridge tonight, then," Conan grinned. Guards aside, they'd really gotten lucky when they stumbled into the watch rotation for the bridge.

They could use their watches to stuff the tinder beneath the bridge. They could even try to scrape some of the coating off the top. And when everything was in place, they would wait until one of their watch nights, set it aflame, and get out of town.

Conan's belly knotted as he went over the plan in his mind again. He knew it would hurt Alannah. But, in his experience, someone always got hurt in relationships because they always ended. Brian had buried two wives and divorced a third before marrying Conan's sister. Broccan as good as died the day he lost his family. And Conan had been betrayed by his own kin so many times he'd lost count.

Keeping his relationship with Alannah short and sweet, that was all he wanted.

He didn't want to hurt her, but he didn't see a way around it. The bridge needed to burn and if she found out what they were doing, she'd do everything in her power to stop them. Though she couldn't physically prevent it, Conan knew she was both clever and determined—a potent combination.

Conan took up his post on the western side of the bridge, enjoying the way the coming storm matched his own emotions. Ardál stood silent watch on the eastern shore. Conan couldn't figure him out, though this particular night he appreciated the quiet companionship.

He was leaner than the rest of the men, though still built of solid muscle. There was no way he couldn't be with all the training they did together. He was a fair swordsman, but lethal with a spear or a bow. He journeyed with them, ate with them, drank with them, but never shared any more of himself than that. Conan had always thought Cormac a quiet and contemplative sort, but his brother was nothing compared with Ardál.

Cormac commanded any room he entered, whether he spoke or not. But Ardál could make himself invisible, disappearing into shadows like a ghost.

The sound of footsteps made Conan jump. Then mutter an oath.

Walking straight for him, a fool grin on his face, was Teague.

"I heard I might find you here," he called, walking all the way onto the bridge and leaning against the rail.

Conan didn't have anything to say to that, so he kept his mouth shut and pretended to keep watch. He had nothing to say to Teague at all, for that matter.

"Why are you hiding from me?" he asked, clearly unable to just leave Conan alone. "You weren't there when they explained your plan."

"Dallan and I were distracting Alannah and Emer." Conan

shot him a pointed look. "In case things got ugly again."

Teague rolled his eyes. "I'm not some beast whose emotions roll by on a whim. Honestly, Conan. I hated what happened in Dyflin as much as you did." He sounded defensive. "I told him not to do it."

"It's more than just that and you know it." Kidnapping was only the last and greatest of his brother's sins. That list was too long to bear repeating. "Time after time, you prove that you are not a man of honor."

"I'm working *with* you now," Teague ground out. "After father's actions, it was clear that Brian is the better man."

Conan couldn't care less. He'd given up on Teague years ago. Helping them now was too little, too late to reverse the damage he'd done.

"Is this how it's going to be?" Teague demanded, frustration lacing his words. "Will you not at least try to fix this?"

He didn't even turn to look at his brother. "Give me one reason why I should."

Teague slid in front of him. "Because we're family."

Damn. He didn't want to feel anything, but his resolve started crumbling at Teague's words. Not because of his brother, though.

Because of Alannah. Because of the way she placed family before everything else, even herself. Everything she did, every single day, was for her sister. If her brothers didn't come back by the week's end, Conan had no doubt whatsoever that woman would tear the earth apart looking for them.

He doubted he could ever have that with Teague, but it made him wonder. What would happen if he did as Alannah suggested? What would happen if he gave Teague another chance?

"Prove me wrong, then," Conan challenged, smacking Teague on the back. "It's your turn on watch."

Then he got the hell out of there.

CHAPTER TWENTY-FIVE

"ARE YOU ABSOLUTELY certain?" Alannah asked for the hundredth time.

Teague crossed his arms. "I'm starting to feel you don't *want* me to stay here," he laughed. "The accommodations are just fine. Truly."

Alannah wanted to believe him. After seeing first-hand the splendor of the rath at Cruachan Aí she knew the ten foot roundhouse was *not* fit for royalty. Emer had happily agreed to give Teague use of their own stone cottage, his guards having to rough it in the roundhouses, but even the cottage paled in comparison with the rath. Still, she wasn't about to harass him over her concerns.

Emer brought over his breakfast, a bowl of hot porridge with honey and baked apple.

"Thank you darling," he cooed. He lifted his spoon but paused, his eyes pinned to the front door.

Both women turned, and Alannah's stomach fluttered when Conan flashed her a mischievous grin. "Good morning, gorgeous," he purred, striding over to where she stood near the hearth and pulling her in for a kiss on the cheek.

His hold on her stiffened the moment he spotted Teague, and she realized that they hadn't been introduced.

"Good morning, gentlemen," she greeted them, deliberately including the other men. "I don't think you've had the chance to meet our newest guest, Teague O'Conor mac Cahill, Prince of

Connachta." She turned to the prince, gesturing toward each bard and introducing them in turn.

An odd smile tugged at the edge of Teague's lips. It reminded her of a cat toying with a mouse. "Pleasure to meet you, *gentlemen*."

"I assure you, the pleasure is all ours," Illadan answered, though Alannah thought his tone a tad acerbic for addressing a prince.

"Please," Teague smacked the wooden tabletop, "join me."

"We wouldn't want to impose." Conan's piercing stare never wavered from Teague.

The prince broke into a full, toothy grin, meeting Conan's bold stare. "No, I *insist*. Alannah, why don't you join us as well."

"Me?"

He nodded. "I'd invite Emer, but something tells me she'd politely decline."

"Something tells me you're correct," Emer called from across the room, not missing a step as she carried breakfast to the newly-seated arrivals. "It will only grow busier as the sun rises higher."

"So," Teague leaned forward onto his elbows expectantly, "what brings such an impressive group of men to Ath Luain?"

"We perform as bards," Illadan answered. "Though we don't carry that rank."

"No less a noble endeavor for it," Teague grinned at him. "You shall play for me tonight."

The muscles in Conan's jaw strained at the prince's comment. It seemed odd that he felt the need to argue over such a compliment as a request to play for one of the royal family. Alannah placed a hand on his arm, hoping to diffuse whatever about the conversion had him getting riled.

"Of course." Illadan sounded about as happy as Conan looked, but that wasn't unusual for their stern leader.

"Where are you from?" Teague pressed, looking from one man to the next.

"We came from Mumhain," Finn answered. "But we've

traveled all over Éire."

"They've even been to Dyflin," Alannah added. "To my knowledge, we've not had anyone here who's been that far east."

A polite chuckle danced around them. "I was there just recently myself," the prince told her before turning to Conan. "How did you find it?"

Conan met Teague's stare as though it were a contest of who could go longest without blinking. "We were welcomed warmly by Sitric's household. Some of his other guests proved more antagonistic, but they were dealt with accordingly."

The air thrummed with unspent tension. Alannah knew the feeling well—it was just how she'd felt right before she fought off Oran. She leaned closer to Conan, whispering against his cheek. "Am I missing something?"

He turned toward her, one dark brow raised. "How do you mean?"

Beyond them, conversation continued along much the same. The deep rumble of the bards speaking and Teague's answering chuckles faded as her focus shifted to Conan.

"It seems tense." She inclined her head toward the rest of the table. "Like there's a problem I'm unaware of."

"There's been a lot of raiding between Mumhain and Connachta of late," he whispered.

Alannah nodded. That made sense. She knew about the increased animosity between the two kingdoms, but only from what she'd heard through merchants and other travelers. Luckily she'd not seen much of it herself.

Conan's stormy eyes sparkled. "I have an idea." Sitting straight, he waited until he had the prince's full attention. "Teague, as prince you help command the king's army, do you not?"

"I do." He narrowed his eyes, a deep, rich, chestnut.

"Alannah and Emer have two brothers who should have returned home with the other local men who fought to the north."

Alannah's breath caught, her heart racing. How had she ever doubted him? She'd never have thought to question the prince himself on her brothers' whereabouts, yet here was Conan, championing her fearlessly.

"Is that so?" Teague tipped his head to better see her. "I take it they did not?"

Alannah shook her head slowly. "No, lord."

"I'm terribly sorry to hear that." Teague sounded more genuine than she'd expected for a man who faced lost soldiers nearly every day. "I am grateful to them for their service. I wish there were something I could do, but unfortunately if they didn't return—"

"Actually, there is something you can do."

Alannah's mouth fell open. Had Conan really just *interrupted* the prince and then asked him for a favor? She shifted in her seat, unable to find a comfortable position.

"Oh?" Teague didn't reprimand him. He didn't even blink in surprise.

"You see," Conan leaned toward the prince, "we learned from someone who'd joined alongside them that they were transferred into a different unit."

"They were likely sent north to deal with Aodh, were they not?" Illadan asked.

All the men joined in now. Whatever tension had existed dissolved, leaving behind a rapid debate on her brothers. The men spoke so quickly that Alannah couldn't get a word in.

"They weren't sent into Mumhain, if that's what you're asking," Teague answered with a lilt to his deep voice. "But we have men all along our borders."

Conan snorted out a laugh, the most relaxed Alannah had seen him since sitting down. "You cannot have me believe you've put men between you and Midhe."

Teague chuckled again, matching Conan's tone. "No, no, you're right about that. Malachy wouldn't look kindly on being stalked as though he were anything but our ally."

Dallan pointed a finger at the prince. "We're circling back to that."

"To the fact that we don't prepare for a battle against our ally?" Teague balked. "That seems an unnecessary waste of breath."

"Stop distracting him," Conan ordered, tossing a frown at his companions. "I know most of your men patrol your northern border. Aodh may not be actively after Connachta, but he's no ally."

"Says the men from Mumhain." Teague folded his arms. "Brian *is* actively after Connachta and raiding across our borders."

"There haven't been any raids in months," Dallan argued.

Conan smacked the table to silence them all. "God's bones, could we just focus?" He turned to Teague once more. "Send runners to each of the units. Her brothers must be among one of them. It's not as though they just disappeared."

Hope swelled in Alannah, a wave rising so high it threatened to knock her over. Emer had been right. Conan really was a good man.

Teague nodded, laying a hand on Conan's shoulder. His eyes pierced Conan like arrows, filled with purpose and resolve. "I'll find out where they are, brother. It's the least I can do."

Every man stilled. Teague sucked in a breath, his eyes widening in shock even though he'd been the one to speak.

Brother, he'd called Conan. She couldn't have heard that right, yet the blood drained from her face all the same. "What did you just say?"

"He said he's going to find your brothers." Conan's voice broke over the words.

She looked at each of the men. Their gazes slid from her to Conan or the table. "Why did he call you 'brother'?"

Conan eyed the other diners in the room then looked to Illadan, who shook his head so slightly that Alannah would've missed it had she not been watching the entire exchange.

Her stomach flipped, the wave of hope crashing against her

gut like the sea churning against the shore. "Conan."

It wasn't a question. She watched the debate in his eyes, in the way his throat bobbed and his fists clenched. She knew he was considering lying to her.

With a sigh that shook the rafters, Conan ran a hand through his dark, wild waves.

"Because I am."

CHAPTER TWENTY-SIX

IF LOOKS COULD kill, Conan would've been dead two minutes ago, though it was difficult to say whether it was Alannah's glare or Illadan's that would've done him in. That was how long had passed since he'd told Alannah the truth. It was also how long it had been since anyone spoke.

Across the table, Illadan sat so still that Conan wondered if he'd stopped breathing entirely. Alannah had gone the other direction, shaking like a cloud about to burst with rain.

Conan had considered filling the silence with an explanation, but at the end of the day, he'd lied to her. If she wanted to know why, he'd explain. If not, she deserved the honor of the full truth. To Conan's surprise, Illadan cracked first.

"Outside." Illadan ground out finally. "All of you. *Now.*"

The men stood, including Teague. Conan wanted nothing more than to give his older brother a good walloping, but he couldn't risk anyone inside the hall seeing a commoner punch a prince in the face without punishment.

"You as well, I'm afraid," Illadan said to Alannah, more gently but no less stern.

She looked ready to argue, but Conan knew that wouldn't go over well with Illadan right now.

"Please," Conan pleaded. "There is more you must know."

As they trudged in silence out the back door of the hall, a leaden weight settled in Conan's chest. He'd never wanted to lie to Alannah, but what choice had he had? It wasn't as though he could betray his oath to Brian, betray his closest friends. Yet it tore at him all the same.

The moment Illadan shut the door, Conan jumped at Teague, shoving him hard. "I can't believe you! We give you *one* job, one, simple way to prove yourself and you—"

"I know! I know," Teague held his hands out. He didn't even shove Conan back. "The fault lies entirely with me."

"Speaking of lies." Alannah stepped between them, finger pointed at his chest, eyes on fire. "I *knew* you weren't bards!"

Finn stepped forward. "I am actually a bard by training, though I wasn't accepted as an apprentice."

"Who are you?" Alannah speared them as one, breathing hard. "I'm apparently too trusting, but I'm no fool. You've all been lying. Who are you?"

"I'm Teague's younger brother," Conan answered her honestly.

"Is Conan your true name?"

"Aye," he assured her. More than anything he wanted to pull her into his arms and comfort her, but he knew it would only make matters worse. "We gave your our true names, but not our titles."

She took a wobbly step back. "Titles?"

"Illadan is the nephew of Brian Boru, son of his brother Mahon, and therefore a prince of Mumhain. Dallan used to be the heir apparent to the throne of Laigin. Ardál is the son of Brian's huntsman. And Finn is as he says, a highly accomplished bard who should've trained with the masters, though he is also one of the best swordsmen I've met."

Conan watched Alannah's face change as she digested it all. He could hardly hear anyone breathe, let alone move. "Why are there two princes hiding in my inn?"

"We are oathsworn to Brian, King of Mumhain," Conan began.

Illadan stepped forward, but Conan held a hand out to stop him.

"Brian came to visit Cahill in peace. He brought us in case things got out of hand, but we were to keep attention away from ourselves."

"By performing in front of the entire town?"

Dallan took up in his defense. "The best place to hide is where folks least expect it. In this case, in plain sight."

"How could you?" Her voice cracked, breaking like his resolve had only minutes earlier. "How could you lie to me? Why didn't you trust me?" The words sounded so small that they hurt him all the more.

"I didn't want my father to know I was here." It was the truth, but only just. Damn it all, why did he have to climb through this twisted web? He was not the sort of man who answered lies with lies. "Remember how I told you I didn't speak with him?" He swallowed hard, his throat tightening. "That was the truth. I don't want to see him. Ever."

"I trusted you." Her narrow nose flared, her lips rolling in on themselves. "I never should have trusted you."

Conan's heart sped as panic settled in his chest. "Alannah, please. I didn't want to lie to you, but I swore an oath. I must keep my word."

He couldn't decide if she was about to run him through with her sword or burst into tears. What was worse, he couldn't decide which would upset him more.

"Then you can keep your word under someone else's roof. You're no longer welcome here." She spun on her heels, reaching for the door.

"Alannah." Illadan moved quickly, pressing the door closed. "I realize that we have hurt you, and I'm sorry for it. But I must request that no one else learn our true identities. Do I have your word?"

She glared past Illadan and straight into Conan's soul. "Aye. I'll never speak a word about you."

Every muscle in Conan's body screamed to follow her, to tell her everything, to make her understand that he'd never wanted any of this. Instead his feet rooted into the hard-packed earth and he watched her disappear into the hall.

"I know you're plotting my demise," Teague began, his hand still resting on Conan's tense shoulder, "but it was an accident. Perhaps when I discover what happened to her brothers, you can use that bit of news to get her speaking with you again."

As much as he wanted to blame it all on Teague, Conan knew it wasn't entirely his brother's fault. "She's been questioning our story from the moment we arrived," Conan growled, shrugging out from Teague's hand. "I've lied to her every day we've been here. I don't think even that will be enough to fix it."

And it shouldn't be. He deserved every ounce of her disdain, her disappointment. He betrayed her.

And he deserved every single consequence of that.

"Let's get our things and go pay our old friend Oran a visit," Illadan ordered, his voice tight as he strode around the hostelry toward their cottage.

Teague followed them. "I will cover all your expenses. Lodging, food, ale. Buy yourselves new swords for all I care."

Conan didn't have the energy to even argue with Teague. He packed his few belongings, lifting his bag and strapping on his sword. A clattering drew his attention to the floor at his feet.

The dagger he'd commissioned for Alannah. The one he'd planned to give her as a parting gift, to remember him and to help her defend herself once he was gone. He picked it up, running his fingers along the gilded hilt and finely honed blade. He'd always known that eventually they would leave. He would return to Mumhain and Alannah would stay here with her sister. He hadn't dared to imagine she might come with him if he asked. And yet, somehow, he never felt that they would part.

He laid the dagger on his bedroll, knowing one of them would find it when they came to sweep the cottage out. Then he followed the men out of The Hart's Rest.

CHAPTER TWENTY-SEVEN

CONAN DIDN'T REMEMBER much of the walk through Ath Luain, but he couldn't help but pay attention once they arrived at Oran's guesting house. When he broke free from his haze, he found himself standing inside a hostelry that couldn't be more different from The Hart's Rest.

Built in the newer fashion, the rectangular common area was filled to bursting with trestle tables, benches, and chairs, all positioned around a central hearth. A pair of doors flanked the entrance, no doubt leading to the rooms for rent. In spite of the heat from the blazing fire, Conan felt the need to shiver as he took in the room. It should've been cozy—small and well-lit and warm—yet something about it unsettled him. Perhaps it was the yelling.

"You must be joking," Oran spat. "Why would I give you rooms when you've taken that whore's side every time?"

Conan sprang to life. He lunged for Oran, but Dallan and Finn caught each of his arms before he could knock the bastard out.

Oran laughed, a sound that made the bile rise from Conan's gut. "And why would I let someone stay here who wishes me harm? I don't think so."

"You can let them stay here, or you can lose your hostelry," Teague threatened, taking charge of the conversation. "Those are your only options."

Oran's face reddened. "Who do you think you are, threatening my business? I'll report you for—"

"I am Teague O'Conor, son of Cahill and Prince of Connachta, and you will do as I command. These men are staying here, and they won't be any trouble."

The bastard's mouth fell open, though his eyes still held onto his fury. He floundered momentarily. "This way," he muttered.

Oran led them through the door to the right, which connected to a hallway with five more doors, two on each side of the hall and one on the end. He opened the door on the end and stepped inside so they could follow.

"You'll all have to share this one. I don't have any more."

"I highly doubt that," Conan snapped, "but we'll share it all the same."

"Excellent!" Teague pulled a handful of coins from a pouch at his waist. "I'm certain this will cover it."

Oran's mood changed instantly. His face lit, a greasy smile spreading across his lips. "Aye, that it will."

"That will be all." Teague dismissed him, hurrying him out the door and closing it. "I apologize again for the inconvenience I've caused. Does this in any way change your plans?"

"The sooner we act, the better," Illadan answered, frowning at the room.

It was only a little smaller than their cottage had been, but poorly maintained. Four bedrolls lay on the rush-covered floor. The woolen blankets over them had seen both better days and what looked to be an infestation of moths, if the holes were any indication.

"Agreed," Dallan said with a grimace. "How in the world is he stealing business from her with this dump?"

"It's all about location," Finn replied heavily. "Unfortunately, he's got it."

"How can I help with your plan?" Teague pressed. "I'm determined to make this right."

Conan felt like a caged wolf. He paced the room as he listened to their planning, everything inside him screaming to get out.

"We've got a good amount of tinder." Ardál leaned against the door. "We could get the middle burned and start knocking it down from there if it doesn't catch."

Illadan ran a hand over his chin. "I'd prefer to have tinder beneath the whole of it, but I realize that will take longer than we likely have before Brian returns."

"It would take several weeks more, even if we did nothing but collect wood and stuff it under the causeway," Dallan braved one of the cots, dropping his pack as he sat. "And that would arouse even more suspicion than we've just done."

"She didn't connect us with the fire," Finn said softly. "Her focus was entirely on Conan."

"Thanks for that," Conan muttered. "I'd almost forgotten that I broke her heart."

"Give her time," Teague told him. "She'll come around."

Illadan stopped pacing and turned to face them from the far side of the room. "Unfortunately, time is the one thing we don't have. I think we should do it tonight and get out of here. It's bad enough that even one person knows our true identities. We can't risk any further exposure."

"Won't that make Alannah more suspicious?" Dallan asked. "She doesn't suspect us now, but if the bridge burns and we disappear the same day she discovers we were hiding our identities, she might start putting things together."

"And she might start talking," Ardál added grimly.

Conan rounded on him. "She swore she wouldn't tell anyone. She'll keep her word."

"Even if the bridge she's protecting is at risk?" Illadan challenged. "No, Ardál and Dallan are correct. If she thinks we're responsible, she'll consider her oath forfeit. Teague, we may need you to cover our tracks once we leave, should she get any ideas of our involvement."

"I swear to you, no one will believe you responsible."

Illadan nodded slowly. "Then it's decided. Tomorrow night, we burn it. Take some time to do anything you wish before we leave, and meet me in the woods at midday to get the final piles of tinder."

Conan didn't need to be told twice. If Illadan was giving him time to sulk, he'd take it. He strode out the door and headed toward the river. As he left the inn, he spotted Oran talking with two burly-looking men—the sort who had a good deal of muscle and not much else in their favor. The same two who'd held Alannah back the day they'd run into Brian and his brothers. They stood an arm's length from the window into the Fianna's room. Conan didn't like that one bit, but that was a problem for later. Right now, he needed to be alone and to think.

Putting everything except Alannah from his mind, he sat on the grassy bank at the riverside. The water gurgled at his feet, a gentle current carrying it south, where it would eventually reach the Fianna's stronghold at Cenn Cora.

Footsteps interrupted his thoughts before they could even take form. Conan expected Finn or Dallan, or perhaps both, to have followed in an effort to cheer him. He would never have guessed it was Teague until his brother sat beside him on the dewy grass.

"What do you want?" Conan grumbled. He didn't enjoy Teague's company normally, let alone just after his brother destroyed his relationship with Alannah.

"You need to talk with someone," he answered simply.

Conan narrowed his eyes. "That someone isn't you."

"On the contrary, I'm your best option. Everyone else here has to remind you of your mission for Brian. I'm the only one who can give you unbiased advice."

"And how do I know you aren't trying to manipulate me for your own designs?"

Teague shrugged, leaning back onto his arms. "You don't, I suppose. But it could be a fun exercise in trust. So tell me what you're thinking as you stare blankly into the river."

Conan swallowed. He doubted Teague could have anything useful to say, and he now had even less faith in his brother. But

Teague was right, he needed to talk through his troubles.

"I don't know what I thought would happen when I got involved with her. I knew from the very beginning that I'd be leaving, and even if I wasn't, how could I be with her knowing how deeply I betrayed her?"

"You mean by hiding your identity?"

"No. I mean by burning the bridge." Conan clasped his hands together tightly, wringing his thoughts from his mind. "Even if she never connects us to it, *I* would know. I would know that I destroyed her business and kept it from her."

Teague nodded. "So you want to be with her, but you must leave. Would she come with you if you asked?"

"Did you not hear what I just said?" Conan growled.

"Humor me. Prior to today, would she have come with you?"

Conan sighed. If only he knew. "I don't know. She's very close with her sister and protective of her. I don't think it would've been an easy decision for her. Why could that possibly matter now?"

"There is a way you could make it right, but you're not going to like it."

"What, leave the Fianna and live in Ath Luain?"

"Side with her."

Conan sat straighter, his energy returning. "Against the Fianna?"

Teague nodded. "I'm not saying it's the wisest thing to do, but I do believe that would go a long way toward repairing your relationship with her. She'll know what it cost you."

Conan's fingers went cold. He opened and closed his hands, breathing deeply. "I cannot betray them. I cannot abandon my oath."

"Then don't. You can move forward as though none of this happened. Or, you can change your entire life for this woman. The decision is yours. The only question is: Is she worth it to you?"

Conan shot Teague a sideways glance. He'd not expected

anything close to good advice from his brother. Not only was it good advice, he'd brought to light the only question that really mattered.

Did he love her enough to break his oath for her?

CHAPTER TWENTY-EIGHT

HOW HAD SHE let herself fall for him? She knew better than that. Her gut had told her from the moment she met him that he wasn't to be trusted, and yet she'd continued to throw herself at him. How could she have been so foolish? She *always* chose the wrong man, and this time was no different.

Except that it was.

This time, she'd fallen even harder, even faster. She'd thought of asking him to stay. She'd even considered whether she would go with him if he asked her. Lord, how foolish she'd been.

She couldn't go back into the inn in her current state. Emer would know something was wrong, and she'd just sworn not to tell anyone about the men's true identities. Yet another item on her list of foolish decisions, though she didn't have much choice in it. Instead of returning to her sister, Alannah headed out of Ath Luain.

Through a forest to the south lay another town, even smaller than Ath Luain. Alannah knew that some of the men in that village had gone north with her brothers as well, though she hadn't traveled far enough to ask after them there yet. This seemed as good an opportunity as any.

She started walking south from The Hart's Rest, the distant forest looming across the horizon on the far side of the scattered farms. Drawing closer, she saw the branches sway in a breeze that would normally have captivated her, tugging at her hair and billowing her loose tunic. But even the pleasantness of the weather could not rid her of the one torturous thought that shot through her mind again and again the entire time she walked: Why had she ever trusted Conan?

As she neared the edge of the forest, Alannah heard movement nearby. She stopped dead, praying it wasn't a wolf or a boar. She'd brought her sword, but that wasn't a battle she wanted to fight. Some of the best warriors she knew had been laid low by a wild boar in the chaos of the hunt.

Crouching amidst the brush, she held still, listening. Those were definitely footsteps—a lot of them. It couldn't be just one boar, but it could be a pack of wolves. Swallowing hard, she waited a few moments longer before deciding on her next move. Whatever was in there hadn't noticed her yet. If she moved carefully, she could sneak back the way she'd come.

The hair at the back of her neck stood on end when she heard a familiar voice.

"Grab that one, too," Illadan ordered.

More shuffling and the sound of sticks knocking together followed. Curious, Alannah stood and veered off the path to the right, walking into the canopy of oak and ash and birch. She'd been trying to sneak, but her foot snapped a fallen branch. All five of the giant warriors turned toward her, eyes wide, arms full of sticks and branches.

"What are you doing?"

She thought they weren't going to answer her. They stared, looking from one to another, before Dallan finally spoke.

"We were going to surprise you," he said sheepishly. "As an apology for misleading you. We noticed you were getting low on fuel for your fire, so we collected some for you."

Her skin still tingled, her gut warning her against trusting them yet again. It had been a mistake the first time. She had no reason to give them a second chance to deceive her. "Thank you," she managed, though she knew it didn't sound as sincere as it ought.

"What are *you* doing all the way out here?" Conan walked

toward her, the other men falling in behind him.

"I was on my way to the next village over to inquire after my brothers," she explained.

Conan added his sticks to the armful Dallan already carried. "I'll go with you."

"Absolutely not."

There was no way she was going to be trapped on an afternoon's walk with him. The other men hurried past, politely heading back down the path toward Ath Luain. Conan didn't move toward her, but he didn't follow the men, either.

"Alannah, please. Can we talk?"

"I have nothing else to say to you." She turned, finished with him. Her heart couldn't take any more abuse today.

His footsteps followed her.

"Alannah, we'll be leaving soon."

She stopped almost as soon as she'd reached the path again. "Good."

"Can you just give me a chance to—"

"A chance?" She headed toward him, her patience gone. "I already gave you a chance. I gave you one every time I asked if you were really bards. I've given you plenty of chances. I'm through being lied to."

"You're right. And I'm sorry." His features squeezed into a pained expression. "What can I do to make it up to you?"

In spite of it all, his plea tugged at her heart, threatening her resolve. Would she never learn? As a whole, the men who were interested in her could not be trusted. She needed to end this conversation before she made yet another foolish decision.

"You can leave me the hell alone."

"No," he hurried to stand on the path in front of her, "I can't. I wish it were as simple as that, but—"

"But what? You can't stop bedding me, but you can't be bothered to be honest with me?"

"I deserve that."

"And I deserve to be left alone. It's the least you could do."

"Alannah." His throat worked, his eyes pleading as he took a step closer. "I spent all my life training to fight for Brian. He as good as raised me. He fostered me. I've been oathsworn to him since I was a child, and I now serve him as a Fianna."

"The Fianna?" Alannah had heard of them. Everyone had. The call put out for men to come join the band of warriors had sent several local lads into Mumhain. "That's who you all are?"

Conan nodded. "I owe Brian my life. In every way. Otherwise I'd not have deceived you."

She felt her walls cracking, though they were newly built. "I'm still angry with you."

"You should be. What I did was wrong." He took her hands. "I know that I'm not family, but I would love another chance with you."

Alannah wanted to believe him so badly. "No more lies."

"No more lies," he agreed.

"Very well," she allowed, praying she wasn't making a mistake. "One more chance, but I'm going to town alone." She needed a little more time and space to think through all that had happened.

Conan pulled her in for a kiss, his lips gentle yet insistent against hers. Then he left her to finish her journey.

The trip into Curraghmore went about as expected but not as she'd hoped. She managed to visit everyone before dinner time, watching the sun slowly fall toward the western horizon as she walked back to Ath Luain. No one knew of her brothers. Alannah approached The Hart's Rest from the south, circling around the property to reach the front door. On her way around the back of the inn, she glanced at the wood pile, recalling the men's efforts to restock it.

It wasn't empty. Their piles of sticks sat atop the logs and tinder that Alannah had collected just before they arrived. But she had more than enough fuel to feed the fire for another fortnight at least, even without their contribution. Confused by the seeming contradiction, Alannah continued past, her mind racing.

By the time she reached the kitchen where Emer prepared a rich meal of roast salmon, Alannah put the pieces together.

The confusion when she'd first found them in the woods. The hesitation in answering her question. The unnecessary addition to her woodpile.

They'd clearly not checked her stores.

Which meant Conan had lied to her. Again.

CHAPTER TWENTY-NINE

ALANNAH COULDN'T STOP going over the events of that day in her mind. Not only had Conan lied to her, it had been about wood. Why would they lie to her about collecting wood?

She sat staring into the fire as Emer shut down the inn for the night.

Why would they need wood? And why would they need to hide it from her?

The fire popped and hissed. Then a deeply unsettling thought struck her.

Twigs and sticks are used to feed fires.

They couldn't possibly be behind the fire at the bridge, could they?

Worrying her lower lip, Alannah ran through the facts again. They lied about their identities. They were some of the best warriors in the kingdom, and they'd been assigned to stay in town and wait? That did seem odd, but not impossible.

The fire happened after they'd arrived. They'd helped put it out, but when Alannah rushed out of the inn, they were already outside. Which meant they either heard the shouts and got out the door before she ever walked into the common room, or they'd already been outside.

It was suspicious, to be sure. But Alannah wasn't going to jump to conclusions. Instead, she was going to investigate further. Conan was on watch with Ardál tonight, which meant she could simply walk down there and look around. But something inside her cautioned against that. Ignoring it, Alannah grabbed her hooded cloak and stepped out into the chilly spring night.

Having stood watch at the bridge herself, she knew what roads and buildings were in clear view of the western guard, and which were not. She stepped lightly, trying to stay quiet and in the shadows. If she could make it to the southwestern edge of town, she'd be able to see what they were doing and stay more or less out of view from them.

More than likely, she'd just find Conan or Ardál standing guard. She was probably overreacting. She felt a twinge of guilt in her gut as she navigated the last few buildings before taking up a post behind a guelder rose bush upriver from the bridge.

The guilt dissipated the moment she spotted them. Instead, her insides tangled into a knot, leaving her with a sick feeling in her stomach and the taste of betrayal in her mouth.

They were all there, all five of them. Conan and Ardál stood in their watch positions on either side of the bridge. The other three tiptoed through the waist-high water, doing something beneath the bridge. They would be hidden from most places in Ath Luain because of the slope of the bank.

But from a view right down the river, Alannah could clearly see that they were up to something—something they wanted to keep hidden. Before she confronted Conan about it, she needed to be certain it was actually as bad as it appeared.

The following morn, Alannah headed straight for the bridge. She eased herself into the frigid water, shivering as she waded out to inspect the underside. The last of her hopes came crashing down when she spied twigs and branches stuffed between the trusses. The entire underside of the causeway was filled with them. Dried pine needles, handfuls of hay, and similarly flamma-ble tinder was distributed throughout the twigs.

There was no more denying it. The evidence lay right before her. Her blood boiled, anger coursing through her like raging waters through a broken dam. She grabbed a fistful of the tinder and twigs, pulling it from beneath the bridge and tossing it onto the topside. Then another.

This entire time, he'd been lying to her. Initially, she understood. They didn't know each other—they'd only just met. It wasn't meant to be anything more than a night of fun. Of course he wouldn't have told her all his secrets.

She kept pulling, faster and faster.

But once he'd learned how important this bridge was to her livelihood, he still tried to destroy it. Not only that, but he'd even joined the damned watch to help protect it!

Alannah lost all track of time as she ripped apart their careful work, destroying their plan as she hatched her own. For all she cared for Conan, she couldn't let him get away with this.

Before she did anything too drastic, Alannah determined that she at least owed Conan the privilege of an explanation. She doubted anything could convince her that a plan to destroy the bridge held merit, but she wanted, so desperately, to be wrong in spite of all the evidence stacked against him.

By the time she'd finished pulling every last stick from beneath the bridge, she'd created a pile on top of it so large that it obstructed the road. Happily, few folk had passed as she'd been working. None of them were curious enough to ask about her project. She pushed all the brush down the bridge and out of the way, carrying it by unwieldy armfuls to the nearest copse of trees.

It was past midday and nearing dinner by the time she'd finished moving the pile and washed all the dirt off herself. The methodical, repetitive nature of her project had given her ample time to think on what she would do.

Though she was furious with all the men, she wanted to speak with Conan alone first. If she confronted him surrounded by his companions, he'd be far less likely to hear her out or be honest with her. Alone, she stood a chance of talking some sense into him.

She still hadn't decided what to do about the watch. Obviously, they were no longer a part of that, but now that Alannah knew the responsible party, the bridge didn't need watching.

The Fianna did.

That thought brought her up short just as she came within sight of the inn. If she confronted them, they would know of her suspicions.

If she pretended that she knew nothing, she'd be able to thwart them more effectively. The idea of tricking Conan didn't sit well with Alannah, but had he not done the same all this time? And he'd lied to her again, after he swore not to. He couldn't have betrayed her more thoroughly, yet her heart ached at the idea of facing him over it.

Sighing she dragged her hand across her face. Alannah knew two things to be true.

Firstly, even if she didn't confront him tonight, she wouldn't be able to avoid it forever.

And second, she was going to need help. Spinning on her heels, she headed for Glasny's tavern.

CHAPTER THIRTY

ALANNAH ENTERED GLASNY'S to find it empty save for his regular patrons.

He narrowed his eyes as she strode over to the counter. "Is everything alright?"

She shook her head, waiting until she could stand near enough they'd not be overheard.

"What is it? You look pale as a ghost."

"I figured out who is trying to destroy the bridge," she whispered. "It's the bards."

His pale green eyes shot open, his bushy brows raised nearly to his hairline. "What? But why? How do you know?"

Alannah told him everything she'd discovered, including their true identities, hating how bad it sounded. Conan had lied to her not once, but twice. And it was the second lie—the lie of omission about coming to Ath Luain to burn the bridge—that Alannah felt justified breaking her oath of silence. When she finished he blew out a long, haggard breath.

"I still don't understand why they'd do such a thing, though," he sighed.

"They came here to do it," Alannah replied, speaking aloud the only conclusion she'd reached. "Which means it has something to do with their king and his politics."

It was the only explanation that made any sense, though she couldn't imagine what a simple bridge had to do with anything important enough to merit their interference.

"I moved all their tinder, so they will need more time before they can light it. But we need time to come up with a way to stop them."

Glasny nodded, his fingers working through his short, thick beard. "I'll fetch everyone here for a meeting. Can't risk it at the hostelry. We'll decide then what's to be done."

"I'm going to go check in with Emer so she knows I'm alright." Alannah called as she headed out the door. "I'll be back soon."

Alannah hurried from the alehouse and across the bridge. The watch on it hadn't begun yet, though she knew the men would be there soon. Not wanting to risk running into them, she took the long way around the center of town. She wasn't ready to face Conan, not yet.

When she reached The Hart's Rest, Alannah found Emer tidying up two of the larger tables while folk finished eating at the rest. The moment her sister spotted her, she fisted her hands to her hips like an angry mama—all the more amusing since Alannah had been the one to help raise her.

"There you are!" Emer tsked. "Where have you been? I was getting worried. The men weren't at dinner or breakfast, and now their cottage is empty of their things."

Alannah didn't stop walking until she reached her sister, pulling her into a hug. "I need to speak with you in the kitchen," she whispered.

Emer's dark eyes narrowed, but she complied. Alannah helped her carry a load of dirty dishes and dinner scraps back, setting everything down before she told Emer the same story she'd just shared with Glasny.

Her sister's hand covered her gaping mouth, her brows furrowing deeper with every new detail. "But that cannot be," she gasped. "They've been so kind."

"I wish it weren't true, believe me. But it is, and we can't let them destroy it."

Emer worried her lower lip, a sign that she knew something

and wasn't saying. Her dear sister couldn't hide a single thing she thought.

"What are you not saying?" Alannah pressed. She needed to get back to the tavern.

"They left this," Emer replied, walking over to the kitchen and pulling a dagger from behind her table.

Alannah went cold. "What?"

"I found it in their cottage, laid out like it was meant to be found," she explained. "It didn't seem odd to me then, but after what you've said—"

Alannah took the dagger into her clammy hands. It was beautiful. The gold handle was engraved with a deer curled up to sleep—the same picture as the inn's sign. The Hart's Rest. Turning it over, the other side held the image of a harp.

Deep in her bones, Alannah knew it was a parting gift. He'd said they were leaving soon, hadn't he?

"They're going to do it tonight." Alannah didn't have much time. "I need to go."

With a quick farewell to Emer, Alannah sprinted back toward the bridge, praying a plan would form as she ran.

"WHAT DO YOU mean it's *gone*?" Illadan growled at the three men hidden beneath the bridge.

"I mean that it is no longer here," Dallan retorted. "There's nothing. No sticks, no hay, no leaves. It's as though we never did any of it."

"Did it fall into the river?" Conan asked.

"No sign of it anywhere," Ardál answered.

A sinking feeling settled in the pit of Conan's stomach. "Someone must have found it." And he thought he knew who.

Alannah had stumbled upon them collecting the last of the tinder. Perhaps Dallan's clever excuse hadn't been as convincing as they'd thought, even though they'd left some of the wood on her pile.

"You think she figured it out." Illadan had clearly drawn the same conclusion.

"She caught us in the forest," Conan said. "I don't think it's out of the question."

"It doesn't matter," Finn interrupted. "No matter who moved it, we need to get this finished and get out of here."

Illadan nodded. "Ardál, have a quick run up and down the nearby banks to see if you can find any of the tinder. You two get started lighting it from underneath."

Ardál took off down the western bank. Finn and Dallan stepped toward the water and Conan followed Illadan onto the causeway. Then all hell broke loose.

Shouts erupted around them, followed by shadowed figures rushing the bridge. Three here, four there. Once they came close enough, Conan could make out the members of the watch that Alannah assembled to guard the bridge. The vengeful angel herself stormed toward him, dagger in hand.

Conan didn't want to fight them. They were so few in number, though, that he and the Fianna could hopefully disarm them without doing much harm.

"So much for keeping our involvement a secret," Dallan muttered from a few feet away. "At this rate, the entire town will be able to tell Cahill exactly what had happened to the causeway."

"You will step away from the bridge and get out of our town," Alannah demanded, loud enough for all to hear. She had no lack of bravery, he'd give her that.

"We cannot." Conan's chest felt as though it would shatter into a thousand tiny shards.

"Why?" she cried, her voice breaking. "Why must you destroy it? What cause could that possibly serve?"

Conan turned to Illadan. He wasn't about to spill their entire plan without his leader's approval, but he'd also sworn to

Alannah that he wouldn't lie to her again.

Illadan pinched the bridge of his nose. "You may as well just tell her."

"Your king built the bridge as a blockade, not to help travelers cross the river," Conan explained. "He did it to incite Brian to rash action."

"And it appears he has succeeded," Alannah shot back, crossing her arms.

"We were meant to remain hidden," Conan swallowed. "Obviously, that has gone awry."

"You have told me nothing but lies since the moment we met." She took a step forward.

Conan caught her furious gaze. "And I deserve every ounce of your anger for it."

"Will you not yield?" she begged. "You know how important this bridge is to our town."

"I wish that we could, but we must destroy it." Illadan lifted his voice, addressing the crowd at large that had gathered. "You should go home. We do not wish to harm you, and this is a fight you cannot win."

As if to emphasize that point, Teague stepped over to stand beside Conan. "I'm sorry, Alannah, but this is a matter of great political weight."

A hole opened in Conan's chest when he saw the look of disbelief that washed over Alannah. But she recovered quickly, tightening the grip on her dagger and unsheathing her sword.

Conan swallowed hard, hesitating. The doubt that had begun when he first realized how much he cared for Alannah sprang up with renewed vigor. Was he on the right side here? All oaths and lies aside, she made a fair point. Was the political situation here actually more important than the impact of the bridge on the people of Ath Luain? For the first time since he'd joined the Fianna, Conan felt that he stood on the wrong side of the cause.

Teague's suggestion swirled through the chaos of his thoughts. Before he could think better of it. Conan walked over to Alannah and turned to face off against the Fianna.

CHAPTER THIRTY-ONE

"WHAT THE HELL are you doing?" Illadan shouted, fury etched into his features.

"What I should have done sooner." Conan looked at Alannah, her sky blue eyes wide in shock.

Teague grinned at Conan, moving beside him. "If the Fianna are divided, then I must choose a side. And I stand by my brother."

Illadan swore, the only time Conan had heard him do so. Finn and Dallan stared at Conan in disbelief.

"Conan, be reasonable," Illadan ordered. "Are you truly prepared to break your oath over this?"

That question should terrify him. It should make him reconsider his decision. But it didn't. A blanket of calm descended around him and with it, clarity. He answered without hesitation.

"I am."

Illadan's face fell as he drew his sword, nodding for Dallan and Finn to carry on with the plan.

Conan charged them, intending to block them from lighting the causeway, but Illadan moved in his way. His sword came down in a blow that would have severed Conan's neck had he not blocked it.

Finn and Dallan dove in, shouting. Finn grabbed Illadan. Dallan took hold of Conan.

Illadan glared at him. "Conan, no matter your skill you can't fight all of us at once."

"He's not fighting you alone," Alannah ran toward them, Teague and his men right behind her.

"Stop it, all of you!" Ardál yelled, sprinting back down the bank toward them. "We have bigger problems than Conan's divided loyalties."

Before Conan could question him, the crowd around them started shouting. From the bridge, the sound of swords clashing echoed over the moonlit water. A scream followed, then another. Conan's breath caught as the causeway ignited somewhere near its center.

Alannah swore, charging across the bridge.

"Who's out there?" Conan called. He and the other Fianna followed only steps behind her.

"Glasny," she called over her shoulder as she ran.

They'd not gotten far when Glasny met them, bleeding and panting. The moment he reached Alannah, he placed a hand on her shoulder and bent to catch his breath. Sweat plastered his auburn hair to his red face, dripping in beads over his cheeks. A quick assessment told Conan his wounds weren't mortal, though the gash on his thigh would need treating to keep it from festering. He'd hate to see the man lose a leg, or worse.

"What happened?" Alannah looked from Glasny to the burning bridge half a mile in front of them. "Are you alright?"

"I came around from the other side, just as you said. When I reached the center, I found Oran's friends dumping oil. I tried to stop them, but my swordskill isn't what it used to be."

Oran had been talking with two men just earlier. Could that have been what they discussed? Something about it had felt odd, but Conan had assumed Oran was up to his usual sorts of villainy.

"Oran wasn't with them?" he asked.

Glasny shook his head. "I asked that, when I was trying to slow them down from lighting it. They said he had other plans tonight."

Conan didn't like the sound of that at all. "Other plans?"

A fresh round of screaming erupted behind them. In front of

them, flames the color of a sunset licked ever higher. Billowing columns of black smoke twined about the fingers of flame. Conan shared a look with Alannah—the first since she'd learned the depth of his deception. The flames danced in her eyes, darting like fireflies.

As the commotion escalated all around them, Conan and Alannah pushed past the rest of the Fianna to get back to the nearer shore they'd just left. He could do without all the back-and-forth, but something told him this was only the beginning of the trouble.

They returned to the western end of the causeway to find a group of six men blocking their path. They carried arming swords, their tunics and trews a plain brown. All their faces lay hidden beneath deep hoods, but Conan didn't need to see their mouths to know they wore scowls. It was written in their stance, in their obvious irritation at the interruption.

Beyond them, the villagers who'd followed Alannah to protect the bridge fought against a second group of men, clothed the same as the first. Two men hefted a jug of oil, tipping it to coat the end of the causeway. Three more shoved away villagers who tried to stop them. Curses and profanities filled the air between them, threats of violence backed by the drawing of swords.

They had seconds before real bloodshed would begin.

"Stand down!" Teague shouted the command at the hooded men as he stopped behind Conan.

Not one of them budged.

"Do you not know who I am? Your prince commands you to let us pass and cease this hostility. This causeway is under the protection of King Cahill."

At the mention of princes and kings, the men shuffled. The men on either end looked to one of the ones in the center of the line. But the men facing the villagers hadn't heard any of the exchange.

Conan knew Illadan would have debated whether to help protect the villagers or burn the bridge. Both fell under their oaths as Fianna—to follow Brian's orders and destroy the causeway and to help those in need. When it had been a simple matter of sneaking about to undermine the bridge, when the plan had been to set fire to it in a matter of minutes and then leave town, the answer had been simple.

But now innocent lives were at stake. People's livelihoods were being challenged, and they were fighting back. And the people defending the bridge were not in the wrong here.

The Fianna were.

Aye, it seemed an easy solution to a political standoff, but just as many lives would be affected as in a battle, even if they yet lived. That so many villagers came out to defend the causeway was proof enough of that.

Conan knew the right thing to do as soon as he stood facing off with Alannah at the outset of the conflict. Which meant there was only one way forward now, as the villagers prepared to face the blades of Oran's men.

With a shout, he charged the line of men barring their path. He didn't aim to kill, only to incapacitate. Teague could judge them later for their actions against their king, but he couldn't hold off any longer in helping the townsfolk. Conan easily moved through the hooded men, jumping in to defend the first villager under threat. Alannah stepped in front of the next. Teague followed, a skilled warrior in his own right.

After his pommel dispatched one of Oran's men, Conan dared a glance at the causeway. The Fianna were nowhere in sight, no doubt working to fan the flames that burned in its center. At least he, Alannah, and Teague were getting this side of things under control.

He waited for Alannah to knock out the man she battled, grabbing her hand to lead her back onto the causeway. They still had the fire to deal with—and the Fianna.

She tugged hard against him. "Conan, wait."

"We must hurry if we hope to keep the bridge passable."

"What if Oran is at the inn?" Fear skittered over her face, and

Conan knew it had nothing to do with the fight they'd just finished.

He grabbed one of the hooded men roughly, lifting him with both hands by his tunic and shaking him until the hood fell down. "Where is Oran?" he demanded.

The man didn't answer fast enough.

"Where is he?" Conan shouted, giving the man another good shake.

The man's gaze slid to Alannah. "He's taking care of the competition."

Alannah broke into a dead sprint.

Conan followed her, dropping the man and praying they weren't too late.

CHAPTER THIRTY-TWO

ALANNAH'S LUNGS BURNED as she raced back toward The Hart's Rest. How long had Emer been alone with Oran? Had he been at the bridge and then gone to the inn? Or had he been there this entire time?

Her stomach churned harder with every pump of her arms, pushing her legs to their limits before it was too late, the buildings around her a blur of shadows and firelight. Beside her, Conan matched her pace, though she knew he was more than capable of outrunning her. He'd done so nearly every morning since they'd arrive in Ath Luain.

"It's my fight," she managed, the words escaping on a sharp exhale. The last time she'd fought Oran, Conan had stepped in as soon as she lost the upper hand. She'd never learn to fight properly if she couldn't see a bout through to the end.

"I won't stop anything but a killing blow," Conan conceded.

"Protect Emer." That was the last Alannah could manage without sacrificing speed, and that was the one thing she couldn't afford.

Emer's shrieks rose above the din they'd left behind as Alannah closed the last few steps to The Hart's Rest. She didn't slow to open the door. Instead she led with her hand, the oaken boards shaking in protest as she barreled through. But she didn't stop there. Sword still in hand, Alannah headed straight for the kitchen.

Oran's hand grasped Emer's throat. Her screams died down

as he shoved her back, her hands gripping his in a feeble attempt to loosen his hold on her. She collapsed in an awkward angle across the table, helpless against Oran's iron grip.

He hadn't seen Alannah yet.

She lifted her sword, slowing only enough that she didn't risk hitting Emer should she miss.

But she didn't miss.

Oran heard her just before her sword fell. He let go of Emer, turning and raising his own sword to parry.

Alannah's blade caught his left arm, slicing deep enough that she had to tug the weapon prepare for her next attack. She took it without slowing, without giving him time to recover. She aimed for his left side again. Crimson blood slid down her blade, splattering them both as she swung.

This time he was ready. He parried the blow, his face contorted in a potent mixture of pain and rage.

Alannah didn't stop pressing her advantage. She managed two more solid swings before she started to tire.

Conan noticed.

So did Oran.

"Slow down!" Conan called.

She didn't have a choice. Sweat beaded on her brow and her arms burned from the strain of the weapon.

Oran took the lead, stepping toward her, forcing her to give ground. He kept pushing. His brute strength was no match for her tiring arms.

Pressure against her lower back made Alannah glance down. She'd run into a table. Her ankle twisted as she adjusted for the obstacle, and she toppled sideways around it. She managed to parry Oran's next blow, but still couldn't advance against his attacks.

Oran kept propelling her backward, forcing her to give ground. He was toying with her now.

This time when she bumped into something behind her, Alannah knew exactly what it was. The sudden, searing warmth of the hearth told her things were about to take a dangerous turn. Panic flooded her, seeping like a river of ice down her spine. She needed to get away from the fire before Oran got any ideas.

"Maybe I can burn you and the causeway in one night," he spat, raising his sword for a killing blow.

Alannah swung her hips sideways, leading with her core to force her way around the blazing hearth. She tried to parry, but didn't manage it while avoiding the fire behind her. Her blade slowed Oran's as it grazed her shoulder.

She cried out in pain. Her grip on her own sword faltered, her fingers refusing to tighten no matter how hard she squeezed.

With a laugh, Oran knocked her sword from her hand. His callused palm encircled her throat and he shoved her backward until her head slammed into the partition along the edge of the room.

A flower of pain bloomed from her shoulder, a bone-deep throbbing that reached down her arm and toward her chest. She gasped, struggling to swallow as Oran crushed her throat. Alannah shoved him, pushing his arm hard.

In response, he dropped his sword and used both hands to lift her off the floor and choke her.

Fog tickled the edges of her mind. Alannah gasped again, more desperately, as she fought for both air and consciousness.

Emer's screams pierced her groggy thoughts. Over Oran's shoulder, Alannah saw Conan coming toward them. One look at his face told her he was going to intervene.

Oran just kept squeezing and laughing, the sound as pleasant as a cauldron scraping stone. Conan was nearly to him.

A sudden burst of energy coursed through Alannah, making her ears pound and her chest flutter. She was not going to be saved again, not while she could still breathe. Her hands were no use, her arms too short to do any damage. She needed a weapon.

The dagger. Conan had given her a dagger, and she'd brought it to the causeway with her. Alannah reached for her belt, exhaling in relief when her fingers grasped the rough metal handle. She moved fast, unsheathing it and burying it as deep into Oran's side as she could reach.

Oran screamed out his next breath. His grip loosened, but he still held her.

"Again!" Conan shouted, slowing his rescue. "Until he drops!"

Pulling it out, Alannah could reach around him now that his grip had loosened. She sank the dagger into his back.

Finally, he let go, collapsing to the ground at her feet and gasping, as she had been only moments ago.

"You got his lung," Conan said softly, reaching for her and wrapping something around her bleeding shoulder.

Alannah couldn't take her eyes off Oran. She hated him, aye, and he would've killed both her and Emer without an ounce of guilt. But she couldn't stop the bile from rising as she watched him gasp for a final time on the cold stone floor, her dagger still in his back. The room swam, a familiar watery sensation filling her mouth. Alannah rushed across the hall and out into the crisp night air. She managed to make it off the cobblestones before she threw up the remains of her dinner.

A hand landed gently on her back. "Are you alright?" Conan asked, his deep, gentle voice doing a world of good for her nerves.

Emer wasn't far behind him. She moved in front of Alannah, gingerly navigating the mess, and handed her a cup of water.

Alannah took it gratefully. "Thank you." The cool liquid calmed the fire brewing in her belly, soothing her aching throat on the way down. "Are you alright? How long was he in there with you?"

"You got there just in time." Emer brushed the stray hair out of Alannah's face and behind her ear. "So like you, to worry over me when you were almost killed. You fought so well. I wish Ossian and Osgar could have seen it."

A laugh bubbled up, but Alannah's bruised throat couldn't quite manage to let it through. Instead, she coughed, her throat pinching in protest.

"I doubt they would've enjoyed watching that, no matter how proud they'd be," Conan told them. "But Emer is right, you fought very well. And you earned that victory all on your own."

"It seems my training has paid off."

In the silence that followed her words, Alannah heard the unmistakable breaking of a large piece of wood. The causeway.

She took several slow steps forward until the river was in sight. Sure enough, a line of fire stretched across the Sionnain from the western shore and out of sight.

"No," Emer breathed. "They still burned it."

"It was you or the bridge," Alannah whispered. At this point, her throat couldn't manage much more than that. "I made the right choice."

Emer wrapped her in a loose hug, carefully avoiding Alannah's injured shoulder.

Conan placed his hand on the small of her back. "I'm so sorry."

Alannah turned her full attention on him. Her heart still fluttered like a lovesick fool every time he was near. "Your betrayal hurt all the more because I trusted you," she wheezed. Lord above, she sounded terrible.

"I know." He swallowed hard. "We came here specifically to destroy the causeway, and that is why we kept our identities hidden." Conan took a step toward her, raising a tentative hand to her face.

Alannah didn't back away. She didn't want to. She wanted *him*. She still loved him. But she no longer trusted him. His rough fingers brushed her cheek, sending shivers through her.

"Everything else was real," he breathed. "Whether you believe me or not, I've always wanted you. All the tales I shared with you, all the details of me and my life, those were truths."

Alannah digested that a moment. "I want to believe you."

"Is there anything I can say or do to help convince you?"

"Why did you change your mind?" she asked. "At the causeway. What made you switch sides?"

"You did," he replied simply. "You reminded me of what was important, of what was worth fighting for."

"And what is that, exactly?"

"The people we love."

Alannah smiled, leaning into his touch. "Family is every-thing."

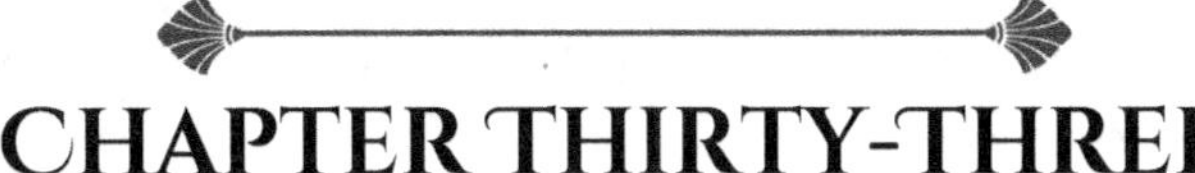

CHAPTER THIRTY-THREE

THE MOMENT THE words left her lips, Conan's face changed. He looked up at her, eyes brightening by the second. "What did you say?"

"Family is everything," she repeated the phrase that had been etched in her heart since childhood.

"What if I make you an oath?" he asked. "I will take an oath and then keep it, to redeem myself."

Now that was an interesting thought. "What kind of oath?"

He grinned, that same, wicked grin she hadn't seen in far too long, and took the dagger from her hand. He cleaned Oran's blood from it with his tunic.

"What's going on here?" Illadan called from the bottom of the path. He looked from Conan to Alannah. "You're wounded?"

"You should see the other guy," Conan told him.

"Oran?"

Conan nodded once, his lips set into a grim line. "He made his choices."

Illadan, Finn, Dallan, and Ardál joined them near the cobblestone courtyard.

"I was just about to make things right with the women, here," Conan continued, placing the dagger against the soft skin of his palm and pulling it across his hand. Squeezing it closed, his stormy eyes stared into her soul as drops of his blood splattered onto the cobblestones.

"I swear that I will do everything in my power to find your

brothers and return them to Ath Luain."

Alannah's breath caught at his words. Long-abandoned hope rose within her chest. "Do you really think you could find them?"

"I don't know." Conan took a step toward her. "I'll need Brian's permission to do it, and it could take a long time. But if they can be found, I will do so. It's the least I can do after all we've put you both through."

Alannah heard the sound of a sheath releasing a blade. Turning, she found that Dallan had also drawn his own dagger.

"You'll have better luck if we do it together. And, as Conan said, it's the least we can do to make all this up to you." He drew the blade across his palm, an angry red river flowing in its wake. "I swear to find your brothers and bring them home, if it is within my power to do so."

Conan and Dallan looked toward the other three men. Illadan pinched the bridge of his nose, something Alannah noticed him do often. Then he drew his own dagger. They all swore the same oath. When they'd finished, Illadan stepped forward.

"I speak on behalf of those not present as well," he told Alannah. "Cormac, Diarmid, and Broccan will aid you. You have their oaths through me."

Tears slid down her cheeks, her eyes blurring through watery rims. "Thank you," she whispered, wincing at the sound of her damaged voice.

"Gods," Finn breathed. "What happened in there?"

Conan placed a hand on her uninjured shoulder. "Alannah proved that all that time training with us was time well spent. She single-handedly defeated Oran."

"And took quite the beating along the way, it would seem." Dallan stepped closer. "May I? My wife's a healer. I haven't her skill, but I know more than these louts."

Another laugh threatened, but Alannah squashed it into a smile instead, nodding her consent.

He lifted her chin, gently turning her head one way, then the other as he inspected her neck. "You're going to have some wicked bruises."

"Will my voice return?" she croaked.

Dallan nodded. "I think so. If it doesn't, you should return to Cenn Cora with us so Niamh can have a look."

Alannah nodded, daring a glance at Conan. Would she go if he asked her?

Would he ask her?

WHAT WAS THAT look? Alannah's face had softened when Dallan mentioned her coming home with them. Did that mean she wanted to? This wasn't the time or place to ask her, of course, but Conan knew he'd never forgive himself if he didn't. Tomorrow. He would ask her tomorrow.

"He's right," Conan agreed. "You'd be in good hands with her."

"The best," Dallan corrected, looking down his nose at Conan comically. "She'd be in the *best* hands with her."

While they jested and Dallan took a closer look at Alannah's shoulder wound, Conan caught sight of his brother making his way toward them. Wanting to speak with him privately, Conan hurried to intercept Teague.

A deep furrow etched into Teague's brow. "Is Emer alright?"

Conan nodded. "Aye. We arrived just in time." He told Teague the entire story, from how they found Emer in Oran's clutches, to how Alannah fought him off herself and nearly died. When he'd finished, Teague frowned, rubbing his beard thoughtfully.

"I'll waive the fine, of course," he said. "The killing was in self-defense. In payment for the attack on Emer, Oran's kin will owe the fine for assault, to be paid either in silver or in the gifting of the hostelry to her."

Conan took a step back. "Oran's hostelry?" That was a massive overpayment of the fine, should they choose that route.

"It's possible they have no interest in managing it and would rather keep their silver," Teague shrugged.

"Teague," Conan began, taking a deep breath, "I want to thank you for all you've done tonight. You stood by me, even though it was a risk." He extended his hand. "Let's consider this a new beginning. A clean slate. All our mistakes are in the past."

Teague beamed at him, the smile going straight from his lips to his umber eyes as he took Conan's hand. "A new beginning it is."

One bridge rebuilt. One more to go.

Conan and Teague rejoined the others in front of the hostelry. "Illadan?" Conan addressed their leader. "May I have a moment?"

Illadan followed him toward the stone cottage where they'd stayed.

"I'm sorry that I disobeyed your orders," Conan began. "But I'm not sorry for upholding my oath to help those in need. The villagers needed help, and I wasn't about to stand there and watch them be slaughtered. I'm prepared to accept whatever punishment you deem appropriate."

Illadan crossed his arms. "You're correct that the situation forced us to choose between two of our oaths, and therefore your actions aligned with one of them. And I agree, that the villagers shouldn't have been left to fend for themselves, whatever our disagreement with them." His hazel eyes narrowed. "But that's not why you defected."

"No, it's not." There was no use denying it. Even if it had violated his oath of loyalty to Brian, Conan couldn't have stood there and fought Alannah.

Illadan stared at him for several moments. "If you marry her in the next three months, I'll waive your punishment."

Conan's mouth fell open. "What?" He'd expected something truly awful—he'd nearly ruined everything and had renounced his oath, even if only temporarily.

"You also vowed to marry for love. If your actions were aimed to fulfill that oath, I could overlook them." The corner of Illadan's lip lifted. "It's not like the rest of us haven't fallen prey to similar misadventures, myself included."

"Thank you," Conan managed through his shock. "I don't think I deserve that, but I am grateful for it."

Illadan started back toward the hall. "Only a man in love would do something so foolish."

Conan smiled to himself. Wasn't that that truth.

CHAPTER THIRTY-FOUR

THE FOLLOWING EVENING after the dinner guests had retired for the night, they all sat at one of the long trestle tables in The Hart's Rest. The whole thing felt so surreal, that just yesterday the bridge had burned and she'd fought and killed Oran. Yet here they sat, laughing and talking just as they had the first night they'd arrived at the hostelry.

This night, however, Teague joined them. Conan had told her that he'd decided to give his brother another chance, to try to mend their relationship. Brian still hadn't returned from the north with the other kings, so the men took this opportunity to plan how they might find her brothers.

Teague had called his own men to help clean the common room after her battle with Oran, a kindness she'd not soon forget. He'd also waived the fine she owed for killing a man.

"Emer," he grinned during a lull in the conversation, "I almost forgot. Oran's relatives would like to keep their silver. His guesting house is yours."

Beside her, Emer clapped her hands excitedly. "Truly? That's wonderful! Thank you!"

Alannah smiled at Emer, but her heart wasn't in it. After last night's events, she realized that as much as she loved her sister, Emer didn't really need her—not with Oran gone. Since Conan appeared in their lives, Alannah spent less and less time helping Emer with hostelry. Even though she'd built it with her own hands, The Hart's Rest was Emer's child, not Alannah's.

Not anymore.

Dallan's casual comment from last night had played through her mind ever since, the idea that she might accompany them when they returned to Cenn Cora. Now all she had to do was figure out how Conan felt about it.

"That place is a dung heap," Dallan told them. "It'll take some work to get it to your standards."

Emer's grin tightened adorably. "That sounds like a challenge I'd be happy to accept. If you lot bring my brothers back I can put them to work, too."

"You might smile a lot, but I sense that you could be a bit of a tyrant given the right situation," Dallan teased.

"You have no idea," Alannah laughed, her throat aching at the effort.

Not long after, they stood to turn in for the night. Conan approached her, leading her out the front door and down the path. They walked in silence, and Alannah fought the urge to ask him any of the hundred questions on her mind. He didn't say a word until they reached the river, leading her to sit down by the bank.

To their left, the decimated bridge stood as a crumbling tribute to the night before. Charred black beyond recognition, only the posts remained for much of it.

"I know that your sister and your business are very important to you." He looked out over the river as he spoke. "And with your brothers hopefully returning soon, your family will be reunited. I would understand if you wished to stay here with them."

Alannah's pulse raced, her stomach dropping. Was he asking if she wanted to stay? Or was he telling her that he wished her to? "What are you saying?"

"I love you. And I want you to come with me when we return to Cenn Cora." He finally turned toward her, his face unreadable. "But I would understand if you didn't want the same."

Her chest filled to bursting. Alannah couldn't form the words to answer just yet, so instead she threw herself toward him, wrapping her arms about his strong shoulders and burying her face in his neck.

His hand stroked her hair gently. "Is that a yes?"

He sounded so vulnerable that Alannah couldn't keep silent any longer.

"Aye," she whispered, his hair tickling her cheeks. "I want to go with you."

He pulled back, his storm cloud eyes holding hers. "Are you certain? I worry you'll miss them."

"Of course I'll miss them," she smiled. "But I'd miss you more. And you travel often, do you not?"

He nodded.

"I thought that whenever you were gone I could come stay with them here and make sure they aren't getting into too much trouble without me."

"You've been planning what you would do?" He pulled her face close, their foreheads touching.

"It crossed my mind once or twice," she teased. "I do have one request, though."

"Anything."

Her stomach tightened at the seductive tone in his voice. "Will you dance with me again before you leave? Like we did at Glasny's that one night."

She hadn't told him, but that had been the best night of her life. She'd forgotten all the things that weighed her down, floating through the night on the music beside Conan. It was an incredible feeling, to forget all her worries and just exist for a while, even if it was only to dance. She thought about that night almost every day.

"I'll always dance with you." Conan's lips brushed hers. "In fact, I'd hoped you'd do more than come to Cenn Cora with me. I'd hoped you'd agree to marry me."

Her smile stretched so wide it hurt her cheeks, but she

couldn't seem to stop it. "Aye," she whispered. "I'll marry you."

Alannah leaned into him with her good shoulder, stealing another kiss and imagining all the dances that were to come.

About the Author

Sophia has been telling stories since she could talk. She loves learning almost as much as she loves writing, pursuing both her undergraduate and master's degrees. She has studied archaeology, anthropology, and the languages and histories of a variety of cultures. Her master's degree is in medieval history, with a focus on the British Isles. She's been fortunate enough to participate in three archaeological excavations and surveys–one at a Native American settlement in southern Indiana, one at a Tudor estate in Essex, and one at an early medieval ringfort in County Roscommon, Ireland.

After marrying her high school sweetheart, attending grad school, and moving nearly ten times in as many years, Sophia and her husband settled into a lake house in northern Indiana. When she isn't working on her next novel, you can find her in the garden and covered in dirt. They live happily in the middle of nowhere with two little boys, two atrociously rude doggos, and one ornery cat.

Facebook:
facebook.com/SophiaNyeWrites

Instagram:
instagram.com/sophianyewrites

TikTok:
tiktok.com/@sophianyewrites

BookBub:
bookbub.com/authors/sophia-nye